from Stephanie
christmas 1988

Memories and Hallucinations

By the same author

Memories and Hallucinations

A MEMOIR

D. M. Thomas

VIKING

VIKING
Published by the Penguin Group
Viking Penguin Inc., 40 West 23rd Street,
New York, New York 10010, U.S.A.
Penguin Books Ltd, 27 Wrights Lane,
London W8 5TZ, England
Penguin Books Australia Ltd, Ringwood,
Victoria, Australia
Penguin Books Canada Limited, 2801 John Street,
Markham, Ontario, Canada L3R 1B4
Penguin Books (N.Z.) Ltd, 182–190 Wairau Road,
Auckland 10, New Zealand

Penguin Books Ltd, Registered Offices:
Harmondsworth, Middlesex, England

First American Edition
Published in 1988 by Viking Penguin Inc.

1   3   5   7   9   10   8   6   4   2

Poems and prose passages by the author are from *Isis* Magazine; *Personal and Possessive* (Outposts); *The White Hotel* (Copyright © D. M. Thomas, 1981; Viking Penguin Inc.); *Dreaming in Bronze* (Secker & Warburg); and *Selected Poems* (Copyright © D. M. Thomas, 1983; Viking Penguin Inc.) and are reprinted with permission. Chapters 11 and 12 are for the most part an amended, shortened version of passages in *Swallow* (Copyright © D. M. Thomas, 1984; Viking Penguin Inc.)
Grateful acknowledgment is made for permission to reprint excerpts from the following copyrighted works:
"Purgatory" from *Collected Plays* by W. B. Yeats. Copyright 1934, 1952 by Macmillan Publishing Company. Copyright renewed 1962 by Bertha Georgie Yeats and 1980 by Anne Yeats. By permission of Macmillan Publishing Company.
"The Death of the Hired Man" from *The Poetry of Robert Frost* edited by Edward Connery Lathem. Copyright 1936 by Robert Frost. Copyright © 1964 by Lesley Frost Ballantine. Copyright © 1969 by Holt, Rinehart and Winston. By permission of Henry Holt and Company, Inc.

Library of Congress Cataloging in Publication Data
Thomas, D. M.
Memories and hallucinations.
1. Thomas, D. M.—Biography. 2. Novelists, English—
20th century—Biography. I. Title.
PR6070.H58Z47   1988   823'.914 [B]   88-40106
ISBN 0-670-82357-0

Printed in the United States of America by
Arcata Graphics, Fairfield, Pennsylvania
Set in Bembo
Designed by Sarah Vure

Acknowledgements

To avoid possible embarrassment, I have changed the names of some people who appear incidentally.

My deepest thanks must go to members of my family referred to in this book, for their generosity and understanding.

For Caitlin, Sean and Ross,
Denise and Maureen

Contents

Memories and Hallucinations

ONE

Parents

I have become terrified of art. It is the fatal Oedipal crossroads where dreams, love and death meet. Pasternak's Zhivago reflected that art is always meditating upon death, and thereby creating life. But the opposite is equally true.

A few years ago, in Oxford, I visited Pasternak's sister, Lydia. A crumbling, gloomy Victorian house; its owner a crumbling, tiny, stooped old woman wearing pumps, baggy trousers and a loose moth-eaten sweater. She took me first to the kitchen to make me coffee. A jar of instant, and two cracked white cups. Our conversation limped. I couldn't connect her with Boris, the creator of Zhivago and Lara. At last she enquired if I would like to see some of her father's paintings. Gratefully I said yes. I followed the pumps and the baggy trousers upstairs. She threw open a door. A blaze of colour and light dazzled me, and I gasped. A miraculous gallery. I recognised Tolstoy, young Boris. The floor was littered with still more glowing canvases and pieces of frames. "I'm preparing them for an exhibition." I ghosted after her, round the spacious room, drinking in the genius of Leonid Pasternak. For several minutes I stood before the portrait of a beautiful, dreamy young woman brushing her long hair. I fell in love with her.

"Who is she?"

The bent old woman shrugged her shoulders. "Oh, that was me."

Indifferent to her lost youth and beauty, she turned away. Nothing mattered except the immortal genius of her father. I had the feeling that the brilliant canvases had drained all the light and life from his daughter's house.

"I hope you've got these insured," I said.

"No. If anyone stole them, what could replace them?"

We returned to the cellar kitchen, and she showed me family photographs, mostly of Boris and his children. One of the sons, her nephew Lyovya, had died in eerie circumstances, she told me. In his thirties and in perfect health, he dropped dead of a heart attack on that same Moscow street on which Yuri Zhivago had felt the onset of his fatal attack.

Did Pasternak have an unconscious premonition? Did his son's heart stop beating because it remembered what had happened, fictionally, in that street? Or was it blind chance? I give the questions to Rozanov in *Swallow*, but they were really my questions; the Soviet poet plagiarised me.

I can't help thinking Pasternak's genius turned his son into a shade, just as Lydia became a shadow in face of her father's art.

I am frightened by the coincidences that seem to cluster around art—even bad art or non-art. Once, I was reading to a class of students a poem I'd written about a nestling. Our cat, grey Lucina, had mauled the baby bird before we could interfere. The poem was new, I thought it better than it was; it would later go into the wastepaper basket. As I was reading the weak verses to my class, my voice full of compassion and vanity, there was a knock on the classroom door. One of my colleagues entered, his hands cupped around something tiny. "I found this outside," he explained, in a troubled voice; "can anyone suggest what I can do with it?" My students gasped; he was showing us an injured nestling.

The students thought it was a put-up job. As though we'd have conspired to maim a nestling in order to amaze them. No one knew what he could do with it. He took it back out to the carpark, laid it gently on the tarmac, jumped into his car, tried several times to drive a tyre over it and eventually succeeded. Then he got out of the car and vomited.

I sink on to the couch and stare at a patch of grey sky through a grimy window. I hear my analyst settle into her chair behind my head. My stomach starts rumbling, as it always does during our sessions.

"I didn't want to come today."

A slight pause; a clearing of her throat. "Why is that?"

"Because I feel better—more cheerful—and I don't want to get myself depressed again."

"Well, you needn't always talk about things that depress you."

I chuckle lightly in response to her amused tone. "No, I suppose not."

"Tell me why you feel more cheerful."

"Well, it's mainly because the trip to Munich went quite well. I found I could still give a reading, and cope with the travel, which gave my morale a boost. I actually enjoyed the couple of days; it's the first time I've enjoyed anything for a year."

"Good."

"The weather was good, quite spring-like, and I enjoyed strolling around. My hosts pointed me towards a cathedral, but instead I found a sex shop. I bought the filthiest magazine I could find. It had photos of men and women pissing over each other. And even defecating. I don't fantasise about that sort of thing, but I found the magazine exciting. I suppose it's childish; and in a way it appealed to me because it was childlike. A total release from inhibitions, a total breakdown of barriers between people."

Her disembodied voice doesn't intervene. I can hear her thinking, thinking.

"All the same," I continue, "it's pretty revolting, when you think of it. I dumped a record I was given of organ music from Passau, but brought home the porno magazine."

And trembled as I lurched through Nothing to Declare, as if I was carrying heroin.

I visualise, while staring at my analyst's ceiling, the surprisingly crowded Munich hall. In a building called the Gasteig. I mis-heard it as Gastein, and it reminded me of Freud. I give a start. "I've just thought," I exclaim. "This is so like what happened in Freud's analysis of Lisa, in *The White Hotel*! She came back from a few days' break, feeling much more cheerful."

"And then what?"

"Then she had a relapse." I chuckle hollowly. "But she does start to get better."

A silence, in which I fold and unfold my hands.

"So, instead of going to the cathedral you went to a sex shop."

"That's right."

"You weren't a good boy."

"No."

Mother's melodious voice, her warm face: "Now be a good boy . . ."

But my analyst is nothing like my mother; she is tall and slim, her hair greying slightly, controlled, formidably intelligent, impeccably middle-class English in her plain country casuals.

"I still have only a vague impression of your mother," she remarks.

Well, I *thought* I had a clear impression of her, but now I'm not so sure.

The calm disembodied voice tells me she's been reading my poems. And one, in particular, has struck her: *Smile*.

> The smile is already there
> in the first snap, let's say 17,
> under the mop of black
> fuzzy ringlets, sitting on the back
> steps of a granite cottage
> in a Cornish village
>
> the smile is still there
> decorative as a film-star
> at the wheel of a Model-T
> (my father in drainpipe trousers
> proudly draped against them both)
> in front of a Spanish-white
> bungalow in California
>
> and is there, in the same white
> place and in the same sunny

era, my sister in her arms,
and is there
under her early-grey hair
sitting on a donkey
on a Cornish beach

and is there
on a bright January day
having tea outside
with her sisters-in-law
and my grandmother
while I stare solemnly
at my first-birthday candle

and the smile is there
under tight white curls
in a Melbourne park,
a plump floral woman
by my plump floral sister
and I a fat youth poking his tongue

and is there, in the last snaps
of my father, colour Kodak,
on a Cornish quay, and is there
behind her glasses, hiding pain,
under thinning white hair
on her last holiday with us

and now that she is dead and gone,
having smiled in the undertaker's hut
so I shouldn't feel guilty,
and now that her death has faded
like the snaps,
the smile is still there,
some poems have no beginning and no end.

"It's a moving poem," she purrs; "even rather a beautiful
one . . ." The adjective falls like a caress, soothing me,

pleasing me; it's the first time she has ventured a judgement on anything I've written. "All the same, I'm interested in what it leaves out. Your images of your mother are all rather pretty. And yet, in your books, there's a lot that isn't pretty; a lot that's disturbing and violent."

"I see what you mean."

"In the poem, there's just a smile."

"Like the Mona Lisa. Enigmatic. Yes."

We ramble on. At the right, the expected, moment, as quietly as the fall of a leaf, she murmurs: "It's time."

"Yes."

With a sigh, I swing my legs off, and fumble on my shoes. I put my face in my hands to relieve tension, I glance askance at her. She does not look at me; her legs crossed, a hand to her chin, she sits thoughtfully. An enigma, Vienna-trained. She stands as I stand, and ghosts through the door. I have learned it's no use trying to prolong our intimacy, even in a light-hearted way. Once, I said to her, on sitting up: "I like your boots." With the swiftest and most withdrawn of smiles she ignored me. She can be anyone to me, only by being no one.

At the front door our ritual never varies. "See you Tuesday (or Thursday)." A brief smile from her. "Yes." And the door is shut. I climb into my car and grab my cigarettes from the passenger seat.

Thursday arrives, and I still feel fairly cheerful as I drive out of town into the gloomily picturesque Herefordshire country-side. I've learned to time my arrival, and my last hurried cigarette, precisely. Childishly, I dare not arrive two minutes early or two minutes late. I park alongside the forbidding grange; lock the car; push at gates that need oiling; cross the yard and ring the bell. She ghosts to the glass-fronted door.

Again the quick half-smile: "Hello. Go through." Her manner wouldn't vary even if I were to turn up in drag, or swathed from head to foot in bandages.

I kick off my shoes and lie down. She settles. Depression settles on me; the expected relapse. My mind becomes filled with death and I spill it out. Mother's death, then my friend's suicide. We have talked of his suicide before, but she wants more details. When I've disgorged all that pain, I break a silence to say: "Death is bloody awful."

Silence. The quiet leaf-fall: "It's time."

At home, my depression lingers. The gloomy, agitated thoughts, the malaise and torpor, the hissing tinnitus. The next evening, the phone rings, and when I pick it up I hear an unrecognised voice.

"Hello. This is Dr Matheson-Muir."

"Oh! Hello."

"I'm ringing to say I won't be able to see you tomorrow."

"That's okay."

Though I'd wanted to talk to her about my mother.

"I can't see you," she continues hesitantly, "because I have to go to a funeral."

"Oh, I'm sorry. No one close, I hope."

"Unfortunately, yes." Her voice almost chokes: "My father."

"I'm really sorry."

And I am, truly. Sorry and shocked. I know, also, that she needn't have explained her absence; she has broken her rule of impersonality.

And it's again *The White Hotel*. There, the analysis was interrupted by the death of Freud's daughter.

Is it surprising that I'm terrified of art? Not that my book is a murderer, but I sense some devil having fun.

TWO

Radium

". . . He was almost eighty; he died comfortably and at
home. Death is still death, but it was in some ways a good
thing."

Her voice is as calm as ever. Does she feel changed, at the
deepest level, as Freud felt when his aged mother died? I'd love
to be able to ask her; I murmur instead:

"Well, that's some consolation. That's what I was trying to
tell you about my mother's death. It wasn't like my father's.
She was crippled, she had passed three-score and ten; one felt,
one couldn't wish her back."

"Yes, I know."

"Well . . . my mother . . . You only have a vague impression of her. How can I describe her? She was born on
March 23rd; she was like an April day, all smiles and tears
—but mostly smiles; and Amy is an anagram of May. She was
like spring, she was a creature of spring. I wish you could see
those early snaps of her: she was stunningly attractive. Looking innocent yet with something provocative about her. My
father's always gazing at her adoringly. I'd have fallen madly
in love with her. I want to be on their honeymoon, their
honeymoon voyage; I want to fuck her, I want to fuck
her."

I stare up through the angled panes of glass at a grey March
sky. If I'm trying to shock my calm analyst, I don't succeed.
She remarks:

"You want to be inside her. You want to know her. I think
she's a mystery to you."

We are all mysteries. *The heart is a dark forest*, in Turgenev's
phrase.

"It's interesting," she continues, "that you don't fantasise being a child and snuggling against her breasts or perching on her lap, which would be more usual. Instead you imagine her ten or fifteen years before you were born . . . Did you say Lola in *Birthstone* is your mother?"

"Yes, mixed up with my sister."

"And Lola grows younger while Hector ages. You wished you'd been older and your mother younger."

"That's true. I came along too late, when her hair was already turning grey. There's this paradox: she was very caring and over-anxious, because I was a late son; yet I can't smell her skin, as I can smell my father's. I can't feel the weight of her breasts, her thighs. That's why I want to fuck her: to feel the weight of her, to see her in a tumult . . ." The clouds break open a hazy patch of blue. "Still, it's not a bad thing, to remember her smile."

A collection of poems lags a few years behind the impulse and circumstances which created them. By the time I held the first copy of *Love and Other Deaths* in my hands, she no longer lived in a corner of the big Victorian house at Carnkie, kept going by the kindness of the friends who had taken over the rest of the house; kept going, above all, by Jesus. Once, she told me, on one of my rare visits, she had been aroused in the night by a tap on the window. She saw a face peering in. At first she thought it was Donald Adams from next door, looking in to see if she was all right. "But then I saw it was Jesus! I could see his face plainly, and I said, 'Oh, the dear of 'm! he's taking care of me!' " Her arthritis worsened, she was taken to Truro Hospital, and there she asked the almoner to arrange for her to go into an old people's home. She was at a private nursing home in St Austell, twenty-five miles from her friends, before I could intervene. I was three hundred miles away, teaching, and waiting for *Love and Other Deaths* to appear.

So the poem called *Rubble* on the virginal page, mother and son sitting uneasily together in the musty sittingroom-bedroom, was out of date. I had used the crippled nestling of my classroom experience:

She is a fledgling
broken on the road
I want to be out of sight of
But alive, or the world will fold.

It is as though the black hole
drawing her into itself
is conditioning my love
to require absence. She knows

it. She is content. There is
a queer radiance in the space
between us which my eyes
avoid occupying: the radium
Madame Curie found, when desolate
she returned at night to the empty table.

My girlfriend and I spent a holiday at Fowey, so that I could see my mother for an hour each afternoon as well as explore the landscape of Tristan and Isolde. An hour of desultory chat; then, aware that I was desperate for a cigarette, she would stretch to give me a hug, crooning, "He's my handsome boy!" and let me go. She seemed contented enough in the stifling home, spending her days exercising her calipered legs, writing letters, whispering Bible tracts, and listening to Radio Two on her transistor. I couldn't bear the sad image of her, left behind as I strode to the car, lighting up.

At the end of my last hour with her, on our last day, she became worried about the storm-clouds she could see through the window. Summer had ended. I would have to drive through rain. "If you get tired, my sweetheart," she said, "stay the night somewhere on the way—like Bristol." I had no intention of doing so; but as it happened my car broke down and Denise and I spent the night on Bristol station. My mother had little sense of geography, and it struck me as odd that she had mentioned a specific place.

It was something for my journal of coincidences, which I had begun to keep. Already I had enough examples to convince me that coincidences are no coincidence. They kept on coming, through that autumn of teaching and writing. Laboriously I was making a literal translation of a long Russian poem, Akhmatova's *Poem without a Hero*, as a prelude to a poetic version. When I reached Akhmatova's last line, I found an uncanny similarity to the last line of my *Sonoran Poems*, a sequence in my latest collection: "Russia walked before me towards the East" . . . and "As if the whole world moved towards the East."

"*Dec 29*. Met Nostradamus' peculiar version of the River Rhône (Rosne) a few moments after musing on my aunt's strange house name (Rosne)."

As the first days of January 1975 brought my fortieth birthday close I received disturbing news of my mother's situation. The nursing home had been bought by new owners; my mother wrote that they were less kind; the owners wrote soon after to say the fees were to be doubled. I could scarcely manage the fees as they were. They wrote again to say she was a nuisance and they wanted her out by the end of the month. I didn't know where to turn. While hiding the ultimatum from her, I made unsuccessful phone calls trying to find her a place in a home further west, nearer her friends. In one of her scatty, affectionate notes she told me she thought she would soon be moving west. I assumed she'd got an inkling that they wanted her out, and would welcome the move I was secretly trying to arrange. Without a full-stop she was asking how Caitlin and Sean were doing at school and saying she had a touch of bronchitis but it was clearing up. From guilt, I always skimmed her painfully scripted letters. January hurried towards the ultimatum. I was no nearer finding an alternative home. We might have to bring her to Hereford for a while. We didn't relish that.

I found time to note another coincidence: "*Jan. 18*. About ten days ago, I joked, in a *Romeo and Juliet* class, about Romeo and Juliet surviving and living in a semi-detached in Wimbledon (or somewhere). Today, in the *Guardian*, Stanley Reynolds, in an article on optimism, referred to Romeo 'moving in with his in-laws, or setting up in a semi-detached of his own'."

On the last Thursday of the month, as Maureen was serving our evening meal, I had a phone call. It was a nurse from the home. My mother's bronchitis was worse; probably I ought to come down to see her. The doctor wasn't too worried; she had the heart of a young woman, he said. But my mother was saying it was time to go; she wanted to be with Harold.

I promised to come at the weekend. I felt anxious, yet also irritated at having to make the exhausting journey, in mid-winter. Besides, there was to be a dance at College. I didn't usually go to College dances, but this one was a French Tarts dance: there would be students in scarlet split skirts and black stockings, I thought. Now I'd have to miss it.

I drove to my girlfriend's flat, a mile away. I spent most evenings there. Soon after I arrived, her phone rang. Denise picked it up, listened, then handed it to me. "It's Maureen."

I knew it must be something important. Moments later I collapsed on to the bed, sobbing: "She's dead! She's dead!"

Denise tried to comfort me. From their few, discreet meetings she had grown fond of my mother.

Next morning, leaving our children with friends, Maureen and I started the long journey westward. Through Gloucestershire, Somerset, Devon, drab towns and frozen countryside, I drove in a dream of grief and guilt. I hadn't said goodbye to her. Her last word from me had been one of my indifferent scribbles. We crossed the Tamar into Cornwall. Speeding through Bodmin Moor and the Goss Moor, I remembered the yearly trips when I'd drive her back home after holidays with us. Always with a mixture of sadness and relief. Dusk was settling on the granite tors, and on the pyramidical clay-wastes round St Austell.

My mother's strong heart had decided to stop beating. It had been instant and painless. She had left the home for an undertaker's shed. She was out by the end of the month. We picked up her worldly goods from the home: four full carrier bags. As I wrote later in a poem, "The makers of suitcases/ Never cut any ice with my mother." I couldn't bear to see her that evening; we continued west to Redruth, where my in-laws put us up. As I was trying to open an attic-window to let some air in, the window fell on to my fingers. For a few minutes, like Vronsky with his toothache, I felt the relief of a purely physical agony.

Next morning I drove alone back to St Austell to see her. She was smiling in the coffin. Sobbing, I begged her forgiveness. She was smiling; the radium was still between us. The worn wedding ring nestled on her cold finger.

The weather, too, was bitterly cold. I bought an overcoat at Burton's Redruth for the funeral. I drove to the homely village, nestling between two carns, and asked an old family friend if he would arrange bearers. I hadn't seen him for years; he too was stiffening with arthritis. I remembered him coming to Redruth hospital, that earlier bleak January morning, his face blenching as I told him my father was on the point of death. "Sure 'nuff?" he had stammered.

I went to Barclay's Bank to draw out my mother's deposit account. She had sixty pounds in it.

She came west, as she had predicted; was hymned to rest in the chapel where she worshipped and sang; then her coffin was laid upon my father's in the churchyard below Carn Brea.

When we reached Hereford, I found a flowery birthday card, saying: "God bless, dear. Lovingly, Mum." And a cross. Her handwriting was shaky.

I found that our next door neighbour had died, during the weekend; also a much-respected colleague at work. The College was in mourning, both for him and because a letter had arrived saying we were to be closed down.

But none of this seemed to matter.

I abandoned my journal of coincidences.

I couldn't imagine ever writing another poem; because I had written my poems for her. It was irrelevant that she probably never read any of them.

I kept hoping to meet her in my dreams, as evidence she was still alive somehow, with Harold; but she chose not to come. She appeared, though, to Denise, on one of our journeys back from a Cornish holiday; she saw her face appear in the clouds above the motorway. "Look after him," she said.

★

"Since I'm not dreaming at present, let me tell you a dream I had many years ago, when my mother was still alive. It was a big dream. I was in Truro Cathedral, listening to a piano recital. It was awful. The pianist was a fat, lumpish woman, and her touch was like an elephant's. Then, while she paused, the Bishop announced over the loudspeaker that there'd been a mistake on the programme; her name wasn't Lees but Orchard, and she was the illegitimate daughter of T. S. Eliot and a shop assistant from Canterbury. He didn't sound at all disapproving. She began to play again, and now she was slim, and her touch was infinitely delicate and expressive. It was a joy to hear her. I was entranced. I was thinking, if Eliot, who was so prim and proper, could father an illegitimate child on a shop girl, and the Bishop can announce it so blithely, then I've no need to feel afraid . . ."

She listens, seeing but unseen. I edge away from the hot central heating radiator under the window, cross my hands on my chest like an effigy.

"Well, I've thought a lot about this dream. I could write a book about it. Truro Cathedral brings back my childhood, of course . . ."

"You don't like cathedrals."

"No. But Truro's is better than most; it's not so ponderous; it's graceful and lets in a lot of light. My mother took me there a couple of times, on holiday outings. Like Lawrence's mother taking him to see Lincoln Cathedral, in *Sons and Lovers*. But there's still the class and culture gap, compared with our Methodist chapels. Audrey Orchard was a local amateur singer. I never heard her, but my parents would refer to her. Miss Lees was one of my students at the time of the dream: a lumpy, quiet, innocuous student . . . The Bishop: I hate Bishops. Yeats's *Crazy Jane and the Bishop* . . . She tells him sex is good, 'For Love has pitched his mansion in/The place of excrement'. So maybe I was right to go to the sex shop. Then, Eliot. He lived a secret life; he got his first wife into an asylum, and remarried behind locked doors. There's *Murder in the Cathedral*, of course; and also his poem *Marina*, addressed to a daughter who is also his Muse.

"The dream is saying, cleave to the illegitimate. Even the Bishop's not so pure as he looks. It's saying, take risks—in your life, in your art. Don't lose touch with common reality —the shop girl. When I took in that lesson, the girl and the music blossomed; the dregs—the lees—turned into a fruitful orchard.

"I had one analytical session years ago, in Falmouth, with a toothless old Jungian analyst. Just for fun. He said the cathedral was my mother, and the dream was saying I should kill her."

"What did you think of that?"

"Not much . . . But isn't it amazing, the power of dreams! Out of the thousands or millions of names in my life, it plucked those two out of the air—to create a metaphor."

THREE

Making Friends

"I dislike Hereford. Neutered Anglicans and inbred farmers. That gloomy cathedral . . . I once wrote to the *Hereford Times*, on hotel notepaper, pretending I was a visiting Russian called Andrei Kravat. I said I liked their little town, but I was disgusted by the public library. I had been directed to a very old, huge, badly lit building, where I found I had to climb hundreds of dangerous steps to reach the library. I didn't know how elderly or handicapped people could be expected to use such a library. And the stock was atrocious: ancient, decaying books which, to my amazement, were kept chained up. In the Soviet Union we had spacious well-lit Public Libraries, full of modern books which citizens could borrow. I urged the City Council to rectify the glaring deficiency.

"Well, I didn't expect the *Hereford Times* to be taken in, but I did think they might be amused. It was a good joke. But they didn't print it. They have no sense of humour.

"A couple of years ago, Denise gave me her rates bill to post at the Town Hall, on my way home. I had a rough idea where the Town Hall was, but I couldn't find it. I put a stamp on the envelope and posted it in the normal way. I'd only been living here twenty years.

"But I loved the College. It was a terrible blow when it was closed down. I threw myself into the campaign to save it. It was a way of blocking off grief for my mother, and I enjoyed the team spirit that developed among us. Apart from my writing, I've been happiest when I've been able to lose myself in a common endeavour. I can understand how people feel when a mine or a steel works closes.

"We'd spent ten years expanding like crazy, to train more teachers. There was even discussion of a 'Box & Cox' arrangement—four terms, or a day and night shift, I don't know what. A million pounds had been spent on a new library, which even Andrei Kravat would have liked. Then, suddenly, someone discovered the birth rate had been falling for several years, and we didn't need so many teachers. By the time the library was being opened, we were due to be closed down: it was mad. Gogol should have been around.

"We were an obvious choice for closure. Labour was in power, so they didn't dare close any colleges in Wales. We're just across the border, in safe Tory country. We couldn't amalgamate with anyone, couldn't 'rationalise our resources'."

"We fought bloody hard; we had Whitehall rocking. They back-tracked, said they'd leave it to the County Council. If they liked, they could close Shenstone instead, a college in Birmingham. Well, Herefordshire needed our college more than Birmingham needed Shenstone! But here was the rub: thanks to Heath, Hereford and Worcester had just been yoked together, against everyone's wishes; most of the County Council came from Worcestershire. It wasn't a fair fight. Even so, several on their side saw the justice of our case and voted to save us. The first vote was a tie. The crucial debate went on for hours; some of the Shenstone supporters had to leave. We expected to win the next vote. But then some fucking wise-guy socialist played a dirty trick: he demanded a named vote. The Worcestershire councillors who were sympathetic to us didn't dare have their support for us recorded, so we lost the vote. The Shenstone lecturers behind us in the public gallery set up an obscene cheer. We'd have done the same; it was dog eat dog.

"Oh, it's hardly Poland in '39, but it mattered to us.

"The next two or three years were awful. Soon-to-be-unemployed lecturers taught students who would never find a job. For us it was like steering a ship to the breakers' yard. Each September the student numbers fell by a third. And of course some of my colleagues found other jobs. Life got lonelier. The only talk was of pensions and compensation."

I stop speaking, exhausted. My stomach gurgles. After a

while she says: "How did you cope with such a depressing situation?"

"By writing *Birthstone*. It was an attempt to make friends. To make them literally, on the blank page. Jo and Hector and Lola gave me a lot of laughs. I probably got more laughs out of them than any of my readers did. Laughter in the trenches . . ."

I never thought I'd write a novel. On the whole I don't like novels. Novels tell us in tedious detail about people who never existed and events that never happened. I knew that some weren't like that; Tolstoy, Turgenev, Joyce, Pasternak—they managed to burst through the fiction into poetic reality. But I didn't have their genius and I wasn't interested in writing the typical English novel, in which a few characters have love affairs, one or two get married or die—and you think, at the end of it, "So what?"

I would never have the patience to describe how someone moves from the dining room into the lounge. I would be driven crazy by the need to differentiate between speakers: 'he murmured', 'she exclaimed', 'he ejaculated'.

Yet—I needed to make friends. Poetry was beginning to seem too bloodless and self-contained. Too neat. Contemporary English verse, including Larkin's, was nothing if not neat. I happened to read, at the right time, Mikhail Bulgakov's *The Master and Margarita*. It was serious, and funny, and poetic, and crazy; and you didn't have to describe your character moving from one room into another. I was very naive, still, to think that you had to.

A dynamic, trendy local minister, the chairman of our College governors, had taught me how to write prose. He had used his blue pencil on my flowery exhortations to save the College, giving them a Pushkinian economy.

Sylvia Plath said that a poem is like a clenched fist, a novel like an open hand. I wanted to open my hand. Above all, perhaps, I wanted to escape. I would try my open hand at one novel—just for fun—then go back to poetry.

I didn't have the courage to venture out alone. I suggested to a friend, the poet Elizabeth Ashworth, that we collaborate.

She was living in north Wales; since I hated writing letters, I would send her instead a few hundred words of fiction, and she would respond. I thought the creative tension might be fruitful. We conceived the unknown creature together; but very quickly I developed a maternal love for it, and wanted it in my womb. I wasn't unhappy when she wrote saying she would have to let it drop owing to pressure from her course of study.

We had chosen a setting familiar to me, west Cornwall, and a 'voice' familiar to her—a female narrator. I felt, whatever feminists might say, at home in a feminine psyche. In fact, I found it harder, in later novels, to write from a male perspective. The narrator is too close for comfort.

A poet writes from his feminine unconscious, his anima. In turning to prose, my anima—daughter of Eliot and a shop girl—naturally wrote as a woman.

In other ways too I followed the creative process that was natural to me. I started not from an abstract idea but from a resonant image. The birthstone of the title is the men-an-tol, or holed stone, high on the Penwith moors. A relic of the Bronze Age, it was said to bring healing if you crawled through it. For me, in my bereavement, it was my mother's cunt.

I would conjure up a trinity of odd characters, sick in different ways, have them crawl through the birthstone—and see what happened. Since I no longer had a co-author to surprise me, I would surprise myself: "No surprise in the writer—no surprise in the reader," as Robert Frost said of poetry.

My narrator, an Irish spinster travelling to Cornwall on holiday, falls in with an American couple, mother and son, who are trying to find their family roots. They come from Grass Valley, a Cornish community in California. Influenced by my parents' early life in Los Angeles, I have always been moved and fascinated by the blend of survival and change which is a marked feature of Cornish mining communities throughout the world. And I myself came home to Cornwall as an 'emmet', a tourist.

Lola Bolitho is ancient and crippled, on the point of expiring. Her son Hector, an astronomer, has brought her to the home she has never seen to say hello and goodbye. He has to carry her across the stile leading to the men-an-tol.

Recently an American living in Birmingham told me she had a friend from Grass Valley called Jo—the name of my narrator. The real Jo had brought her old mother to Cornwall, and described in a letter how she had to carry her over stiles. My Birmingham friend sent her in return a Xerox of the opening chapter of *Birthstone*. The ley lines of coincidence.

Fearing I wouldn't have enough material to stretch across two hundred pages, I decided to explore and interweave two plot ideas: Jo would be a multiple personality, like Sybil; Hector would age amazingly in the course of their holiday, while Lola would become amazingly rejuvenated. Like an inexperienced, panicky cook, I threw every ingredient I could think of into the pot. The result was an over-flavoured, indigestible dish, even after a second attempt at it. But I liked my crazy Jo, uncertain whether to be a woman, a feminist or a man, randy or holy; and liked my atrocious American couple, uncertain if they were mother and son, husband and wife, or father and daughter. I had made a few friends; and I liked them even better when it turned out that no one else liked them much.

Having finished my eccentric experiment, I breathed a sigh of relief: I could now go back to poems. But, maddeningly, an idea for another novel took hold of me and wouldn't let me go. It sprang from my obsession with the lives of Soviet poets, and especially Anna Akhmatova. She had spent most of her life cooped up in one room on the Neva embankment; around her swirled the evil tide of history; she was witness to all its crimes. I would likewise place a woman in one room of a decaying apartment building; she would suffer and endure. She would nourish artists of both sexes, through ice ages and thaws, and keep their work alive: as Mandelstam's poetry was kept alive in the minds of his wife and Akhmatova. All over Russia, Nadezhda Mandelstam observed, there were old women who scarcely dared fall asleep at night for fear of forgetting their husbands' verses.

The book was to be my tribute to women. Elena would be both Russian and universal; her city would be Leningrad and everywhere.

I was annoyed at being gripped by another prose idea. Hell, I didn't want to turn into a novelist. I would keep it short, and try to finish it in one draft. Fortunately I had a three-month deadline. Not long after I had begun *Birthstone*, the *Guardian* announced a fantasy novel competition, in collaboration with Victor Gollancz Ltd. It had seemed worth aiming at; now only three months remained till the closing date. If this new idea worked out, I would submit both.

It flowed along; I wrote for two or three hours each day, in my spare time away from the emptying College; and in three months it was finished. I was surprised to find Elena starting to learn the flute, in the last chapter. It was exactly right, because she was the Muse, all the more powerful for not knowing it. I found my inevitable title, at the end. In the final paragraph, I daringly entered her room and interrupted her practice. I wasn't sure if I had a right to, and I wasn't sure if she turned towards me with a frown or a smile.

I thought *The Flute-Player* would stand a good chance of winning the fantasy prize. I reckoned most established novelists would be stuck with their own publishers, just as I was contracted to offer my next verse collection to Secker & Warburg, so they wouldn't be in a position to take the Gollancz bait. And I thought if there was another 'first novel' better than *The Flute-Player*, I would be unlucky.

It duly won. It wasn't, strictly, a fantasy, but the Gollancz editors decided to turn a blind eye to that. They also thought *Birthstone* had promise, but it would need a lot more work. I agreed with their verdict; yet, somehow, *The Flute-Player* seems curiously dead to me now, whereas I can still read *Birthstone* with enjoyment. The reason, probably, is that *The Flute-Player* is complete in its limited way; whereas the elements of *Birthstone* are still chaotic, confused, imperfect. One may love the crippled child more than the perfectly formed one.

After sending in the two novels, I returned to that other chaotic, confused, imperfect creation: my life. The years of wine and roses at the College were drawing to an end. The very last term had the air of an Edwardian summer. I had nightmares of being thrown into a school again—hearing the buzz of the nine o'clock bell and plodding, in a black-gowned swirl, to a raucous class. I had no idea what to do. But I would have a year's grace: a 'sabbatical' as a mature student in Oxford. Vaguely I planned to study for a B.Litt.; in reality, I was staving off the time of decision.

My subject was to be Problems in Translating Pushkin. I discovered him belatedly that year, through Charles Johnston's brilliant translation of *Eugene Onegin*. It was an eccentric topic for a thesis, but my old Oxford tutor, John Bayley— now Warton Professor—had wangled it for me.

I decided I wouldn't work too hard. I had mis-spent my undergraduate years by being terribly conscientious. Now I would make up for it, in drinking and—possibly—a little wenching.

Andrew, a colleague and close friend, would also be in Oxford, studying for an M.Ed. He too had no idea what he would do after, and loathed the thought of a return to schoolmastering. But we would have some good evenings together, under the dreaming spires. Andrew had the dark, melancholy good looks of a Scholar Gypsy.

First, his wife was to go to Oxford with him; then they weren't sure; then he had left her for an attractive student: she would be with him instead. I envied his reckless courage in casting off; but feared he would live to regret it. Our lives had run in tandem—Leporello and Don Juan; I would listen to his confidences, and he to mine. We had made a virtue of indecision; now—damn him!—he had been decisive.

The last of many midsummer parties at his country cottage faded into late darkness.

I had a dream about muddled taxis and muddled hotel reservations, which I made into a poem, *The House of Dreams*.

It is a honeymoon hotel
visited by the dead and the living.
They share the same taxis, and a fool
has muddled all the reservations.
They love you. They are to be loved.

Since I'd been reading the Freud–Jung letters—

Sappho is there, and Jung, and Freud,
and the girl you shared a train journey with,
who leaned out of the window and said,
"I wish you were coming with me."

The girl had sat opposite me on one of my overnight journeys
from Redruth to Oxford in my youth. I had not dared to touch
her or speak to her during our dark intimacy; we started to chat
only when the train was drawing towards Reading, where I
would have to change. She told me she was going on a holiday
to Sweden—or was it Norway? When I was on the platform
she put her head out of the window and said, "I wish you were
coming with me!" Wildly I thought of jumping back on. I
should have done. I should have leapt recklessly, as Andrew to
his student.

Jung and especially Freud mingled with Pushkin in my
imagination. I wrote a poem in which a young woman in a
black-and-white-striped dress—who would become Frau
Anna—first appeared, with the two great psychic explorers.
Jung could make cupboards bang and knives break; but Freud
was the greater poet, it seemed to me. Avoiding an expected
rendezvous, they passed one another in non-existent trains. At
this turning point in my life, awaiting Oxford as in my youth,
I was obsessed with trains.

Freud dined sombrely with the faithful Binswanger,
And pleaded a headache; Jung worked late. Owls
    hooted.
In their uneasy sleep the two exchanged their dreams.
Snow fell on the Jungfrau. Lenin dreamlessly slept;

The centuries slowly drifted away from each other;
In Emma's kitchen-drawer a knifeblade quietly
   snapped.
                              (Vienna. Zürich. Constance.)

I read in Jones' biography that Freud once analysed a woman
who claimed to be having an affair with one of his sons. The
anecdote gave rise to a tumultuous verse-monologue, erotic
and violent, which I called simply *The Woman to Sigmund
Freud*:

I dreamt of falling trees in a wild storm
I was between them as a desolate shore
came to meet me and I ran, scared stiff,
there was a trap-door but I could not lift
it, I have started an affair
with your son, on a train somewhere
in a dark tunnel, his hand was underneath
my dress between my thighs I could not breathe
he took me to a white lakeside hotel
somewhere high up . . .

I wrote four sections, dominated successively by water, fire,
earth and air. I liked it, but it seemed unfinished; I had no idea
what to do with it.

F O U R

Firsts

Oxford! Baby-faced, twenty, pure as Cornish rain, I cast aside my National Service demob suit for a New College blazer. I was not quite in the position of A. L. Rowse who, in the Thirties, was awarded one of only two County Scholarships from Cornwall; but it was still a privilege for a working-class boy to go to Oxford, and I was determined to work hard. My parents' sacrifices deserved it. Besides, I had a passion for English literature.

I shared a spacious, elegant sitting room with another working-class young man. Bill, my companion, was slightly built, rather stooping, with a Lawrentian beard and quick, nervous Lawrentian movements. The broad windows, two floors up, overlooked New College gardens: we could not have been luckier. Sharing a desire to economise, we refused to buy a breadknife for several weeks: we tore at the bread with our hands. It wasn't surprising that our scout, who cleaned up and brought us hot water every morning, told us without animosity that ours was the untidiest room he had had to look after in twenty years. I had loathed being addressed as Thomas at school and in the Army, so I politely called him Mr Perkins. He was offended: "It's Perkins, sir."

In our short commoners' gowns, Bill and I attended our first seminar, on Shakespeare. The aristocrat of our group, a chinless bespectacled youth wearing a long gown, had already discovered that Shakespeare had been influenced by Boethius. We were in awe, never having heard of Boethius. Our Scholar was eventually to 'fail' with a good Second, but is now a Professor.

Learning that Newman had studied for twelve hours every day, I settled for eight—with five at the weekends, and five hours' daily reading during the vacations, which were longer than the terms. My life was hardly Brideshead; I didn't smoke, didn't drink, ate every meal in hall; tea and crumpets with Bill and one or two other friends was the extent of my dissipation. I didn't need to buy any books; in fact, I don't think I bought a single book in all my time at Oxford. With spectacular meanness, I kept the College Library copy of Klaeber's *Beowulf* for two years, renewing it each month. I found I could manage quite well on my grant, and Bill and I clubbed together for a breadknife.

Lectures, I soon found, were a waste of time; you had to wear your gown, which I disliked, and you could get what you needed in a library more quickly and comfortably. The only unmissable appointments were the College tutorials, an hour a week in literature and Anglo-Saxon.

Bill was finding it hard to discipline himself. He preferred to sketch or write; to his delight, a student magazine printed a couple of his poems. They seemed enviably 'modern'; I tried to become a poet too, but gave up after labouring on a Petrarchan sonnet. My room-mate was also heavily convert-ing to Catholicism, which took a lot of time and energy. It didn't diminish his puckish humour. He borrowed a monk's robe and hood, and told me he was going to haunt the Cloisters at midnight. With his beard, skinny, stooped figure, and surreptitious glide, he looked the image of a medieval monk as he dressed up. He chuckled softly; his eyes, flared like a hare's, sparkled. I followed him across the dark Quad. A late-leaver from the JCR rocked back on his heels, seeing the robed phantom pass. In the gloomy Cloisters he set off to glide around them. From the far corner, hidden by masonry, he let out a groan of terror, and I saw him come racing back across the grass. I had persuaded a friend from Oriel to dress up in a sheet and wait around the corner.

Bill added another hobby to his sketching, writing and Catholicism. One afternoon he came back from town clutch-ing a small magazine. His eyes alight, his soft lips curled lasciviously, he showed it to me. Called *Spick*, it was full of demure girls revealing their stocking-tops, suspenders and pants. Like him, I couldn't believe such amazing, wonderful pornography existed.

I found the kiosk which displayed *Spick*, and also *Span*: scarlet-faced, I gave the lady my half-a-crown.

Bill returned from the Christmas vac with an obsession. He had fallen in love with a forty-seven-year-old woman. He visited her once a week, clutching a hot-water-bottle against the cold bus journey to Newbury. His eyes feverishly burning, he would recount the marvels of their day together. She wouldn't allow intercourse, but he could come under her bloomer elastic. Bill's Catholic conscience was troubled, but a priest told him in confession it was no great sin.

Not surprisingly he failed his Prelims. Showing me the Warden's kindly letter, in which the hope was expressed that he would find 'other openings', Bill chuckled and sparkled —thinking, no doubt, of bloomer-swathed thighs. He was going to marry her.

In my second year, with Bill gone, I had rooms to myself; but they were murky, facing the chapel and backing on to New College Lane. I developed a squint, had to attend the eye hospital. I fell for a dark-haired optometrist who tried to cure my problem with Mickey Mouse images I had to align. She was a Sloane, thirty years before the word was invented, and I stood no chance with her. I gazed adoringly at Sloane students, few and privileged; they were beyond me. I did have coffee with one tall, elegant girl, who stopped me outside the College to ask directions. Looking for work in Oxford, she assumed the first word of 'Don Thomas' was my title. God knows why, because I looked younger than my twenty-one years.

I wrote passionate letters to Maureen, my Cornish girl-friend, ate crumpets with earnest Chemistry students, my neighbours, and sublimated desire in work. My Literature tutor was now John Bayley, who might have been thirty or fifty, it was impossible to tell. At first his stammer was daunting, but soon I no longer noticed it, enchanted by his enthusiasm, brilliance and wit; I rarely left his room feeling less than recharged and inspired. I got used to his charming eccentricity: while I was reading my essay, he might decide to change his trousers. He would wander into his bedroom, leaving the door open, and call—hopping bare-legged— "C-carry on, my dear fellow!"

I didn't get on so well with the Anglo-Saxon tutor, Christopher Tolkien, son of the writer. This was mainly because I didn't enjoy learning Anglo-Saxon; but also his house in Honeywell Street struck me as claustrophobic, too crammed with books. I blotted my copybook with him twice—my only crimes in Oxford. Once I overslept and missed a tutorial. I rang to explain and apologise, expecting a mild Bayley-like response; but Tolkien said severely, "Don't let it happen again." More serious was an essay I wrote on *Beowulf.* Strongly influenced by F. R. Leavis and the savage style of Lawrence's critical essays, I launched into an assault on Prof. Tolkien's theories. I expected his son to be objective; in fact, he was furious. Gleefully John Bayley reported to me on the row, concluding: "He admits you write like an angel; but gave the impression that you were a"—he chuckled, stooped, and curled aside his head in delighted humour—"f-fallen angel!"

I saw little of the presiding spirit, Lord David Cecil. When the English students were invited to dine at High Table, I drank every glass of wine that was offered, as course followed course; and later, in Lord David's rooms, port. It was my first taste of alcohol. Our Scholar showed off his erudition, chatting with his host respectfully, yet as an equal. The others chipped in now and again. But I couldn't say a word.

It was good to see my father's trenched, weatherbeaten face at Redruth station; to feel his warm handshake. We were always reticent. To see Carn Brea, with its castle and monument; then, as the car dipped over Seleggan Hill, to catch sight of the huddle of Carnkie surrounded by ghostly mine ruins. It was good to be hugged by my mother and Auntie Cecie, and greet my other aunts, my uncle and cousin. To sit down to pasty and saffron buns; then impatiently to set off walking up the hill towards Four Lanes, where my girlfriend lived. It was good, when her family had gone early to bed, to embrace Maureen, turning the images of *Spick* into warm flesh. She was still at school; we both fought shy of the ultimate act. Anyway, it was too risky. And it was also good, in a way, to kiss her goodnight and walk down the hill, sensing the sea at the dark horizon, around St Ives.

Starlit or moonlit, the landscape, with Carn Brea looming, mingled with the lyrical image of Maureen, the kisses still tingling on my lips. "Love at the lips was touch/As sweet as I could bear . . ." She mingled the soft-featured, fair-haired good looks of my earlier Hollywood goddesses with a vibrant, plush-fleshed Celtic sensuality. Her diversions while I'd been away, though innocent enough—never more than a snatched caress or two at a dance—tormented me: had she told me the whole truth? Was there more in it? Was I too quiet and academic for her?

Sundays, she came to tea; and afterwards, while the others were in chapel, we kissed, caressed, fumbled on the sofa. Hearing the faint harmonies from next door, I felt vaguely guilty, but the guilt would be swept away in the fever of our frustrated embraces. In summer we would sometimes take the train to St Ives, to nestle in the shelter of a rock on the Island. Once, daringly, we went for a weekend to the sterner, higher cliffs of Newquay. I asked her to marry me. She didn't demur as, in a third daring act, I bought a packet of Durex. But in her bedroom, that night, she changed her mind. I went to my room next door, not sure whether I was sorry or grateful. It was such a momentous event. After I climbed into bed, I heard my name softly called. I went to her room, and sleepwalked my way through the awesome, clumsy, beautiful act.

My father asked me if I was sure; going to Oxford, mightn't I find our two worlds diverging? He liked her; he said to her with a smile one Sunday: "You've got lovely legs". She enjoyed the gentle compliment. I assured him there weren't two worlds. Unlike one of my Chemistry friends, who hated his working-class home because of the culture shock, I never felt any essential difference. "Manners Maketh Man" was the motto of New College; but courtesy was just as apparent in Carnkie, and in my fiancée's house.

The cornfields ripened to gold; we made love as the distant voices, my parents' among them, sang the harvest home. And, after I'd walked my fiancée back over the hill, I spotted a Durex packet nestling in a cushion's shadows. Heart thumping, I sat down and, while continuing to chat to my parents, managed to conceal the packet.

The sexual delight is forgotten; but the lyrical beauty of climbing hand in hand the crags of Zennor, far to the west, still lives.

Marriage was a distant prospect. I enjoyed life as it was. And why shouldn't I? Mother would bring up my breakfast in bed, and I would laze there till lunchtime reading famous, unread poems and dramas, such as *Piers Plowman* or *Gammer Gurton's Needle*. I kept religiously to my five hours' reading a day. I played snooker and bridge at the Men's Institute, though leaving early to visit Maureen. She was pleased with her engagement ring; her headmaster, however, was shocked. He told her he didn't know whether to spank her or congratulate her. Later he was sacked, for spanking schoolgirls.

Returning to Oxford, I buried myself in study, yet couldn't help feeling I had wild oats to sow. Gradually I worked through English Literature to the special 'Modern' paper —1820–1910. The library *Beowulf* grew more and more tattered. At the Radcliffe Camera I summoned up my courage to go and ask the tall, mammoth-breasted desk clerk if she would like to come to tea. To my astonishment she said yes. I sported my oak, for the first time. As I worked my fingers inside her wet vagina, she seemed like a beached whale. She hinted that it could be safe—I could withdraw. But something held me back: maybe love or loyalty. "Well, I suppose it's not very satisfactory," she murmured. "I must have a pee," she said after we'd finished our heavy petting. "It has that effect, doesn't it?" I didn't know; I knew almost nothing about sex. She used the chamber-pot in my bedroom. I saw her once more, taking her to the pictures; but she seemed altogether too big, and I let the tide wash her off.

I sported my oak again when Maureen came up for a summer visit. I took her punting; posed proudly for her in my blazer. Then, the panic of Finals; the train to Redruth again, and a wedding. My mind misgave me at the last moment; we were terribly young and unprepared. Maybe she had misgivings too. At the reception my father made stale jokes about marriage being a case of share-and-share alike: one horse and one rabbit; and that one didn't know what true happiness was until you were married, and then it was too late. I misread 'George & Vi', in a good-luck telegram, as 'George VI', and there was laughter. We missed our train and Gerald, my cousin, had to rush us by car to Truro to catch up with it. We spent our first night in a dismal room near Paddington Station. Unable to breathe, I went out and walked around the streets for an hour. It was a terribly unfair thing to do. Next morning we journeyed on towards the Lake District. Gazing out at the bleak landscape near Wigan, I saw a familiar figure playing on some golf links. It was my Lance-Corporal from Basic Training days. In unfamiliar civvies, he gave me a shock. I recalled his blunt North Country accent: "No one from Wigan ever signs on."

He had said it to a young fellow-Lancastrian, tempted by the extra few shillings a week to sign on for a third year. Maureen and I had signed on for life, and we were still as wet behind the ears as that uneducated eighteen-year-old 'nignog' in our hut. I felt terrified at the commitment; and probably she did too. It seemed to have all happened in a dream. And here was I in my awkward wedding suit, travelling to the Lake District honeymoon; and outside, flashing by, was my Isle of Wight Lance-Jack, in a roll-necked sweater, taking a swing at a golf ball. It was surreal, a fictional event.

I wasn't even sure why we'd chosen the Lake District. We didn't like walking or climbing, nor Wordsworth particularly. Mrs Morley's guest-house was pretty dreary.

We were both, I think, relieved when it was over. I would have much preferred to resume the previous pattern of living, just seeing her in the evenings; but of course I was expected to sleep at her house. When she left for work—she had got a job as an assistant librarian—I would stride off happily homewards, down the hill towards Carnkie.

Soon I had to go to Oxford again, for my Vivas. I assumed these would be a formality; no one had warned me to revise. Literature had vanished from my mind. It was a shock to find I'd been marked down for a half-hour interview. The student ahead of me on the lists was getting away with five minutes. His name was Donald Thomas. A few years later he would publish a collection of poems, compelling me to use my initials. I have been haunted by him ever since: often I am complimented for a poem I didn't write, or my scholarly book on censorship.

I found myself standing before a semi-circle of twenty or so academics, glaring at me, their hands shuffling my various examination papers. I felt sick. After the half-hour grilling, I staggered out, but was almost immediately summoned back in. A female don inquisitioned me for another half-hour on my Middle English paper—a definite weak spot. She dismissed me icily with the words: "I should read a little more about the medieval rhetoricians, Mr Thomas." I have never taken her advice. Wringing with sweat, acutely depressed, I collapsed on to a park bench.

Till then, I hadn't given much thought to my degree. It suddenly became clear that I'd been on the borderline for a First, and I'd fouled it up. For want of a couple of days' revision. It also became clear how much I wanted that First.

A few days later, back home, I intercepted the postman at the gate. He gave me the postcard from Oxford address-up; I didn't dare turn it over till I was inside. My parents lurked, quiet. I turned the card over. 'Congratulations: Class One.' I said, "I've got a First." I rushed to the kiosk outside the village shop to ring my wife at the library. When I returned my father said, "Get in the car." We drove to my Uncle Leslie's house in Redruth; and after, to various friends. "Donald's got a First." I felt more pleased for my father's sake than for mine.

It would have been normal to have gone on to do research, but no one had suggested it. My instinct, anyway, was to get out into the 'real' world, whatever that was. I had decided, without great commitment, to become a teacher. I would spend just one more year in Oxford, getting a teaching qualification.

The course proved tedious and useless. What on earth did 'retroactive inhibition' mean? It meant, if you came into a classroom and found some Maths on the blackboard, you should rub it out, otherwise the pupils might be distracted. Only one tutor discussed the teaching of English in a humane way. I recall a lecture on sex in English. Sex, he told us, was always present—like a lion in the corner of the classroom.

I liked the idea of that lion. I was determined to teach in a co-ed school.

Thrust out of the pleasant womb of New College, I had digs in north Oxford with a public school housemaster and his wife. The school was next door; its stifling all-male scent pervaded the house. I took Sunday dinner with the couple. The woman was kind, in a housemotherly way; but I was appalled by their linguistic poverty. Their vocabulary was limited to about a dozen words:

"He's awfully nice," she would flute.

"Oh, frightfully," her husband would growl.

"Terribly sweet."

I couldn't help thinking of the verbal richness and vivacity of the uneducated Cornish. "Goin' 'ave a game of snooker, Henry?" "No, you! Rather see two cats playin' tennis."

The public school couple made me feel very class-conscious. To be middle class meant being emotionally illiterate. I displayed my Labour Club card in my bedroom, though I never attended the meetings.

The second term was devoted to teaching practice. I was to go to Devonport High School for Boys, in Plymouth. I approached it with terror. At the first school lunch, wearing my new BA gown very uncomfortably, I had to sit beside the headmaster. In awe and fear, I hardly touched the first course of roast beef. I cheered up a bit when I saw the dessert was chocolate pudding, one of my favourites. I helped myself at the side-table, then chose the jug of chocolate sauce rather than the custard. I returned to my ordeal with the headmaster. As I began spooning down the chocolate pudding, I realised my mistake. It was the cold gravy from the first course. I decided to eat on bravely, preferring to be thought an eccentric rather than an idiot. No one was impolite enough to notice. I never recovered from my bad start.

I had digs in Plymouth, and rushed for the train every Friday evening. Occasionally during the week I exchanged passionate kisses with a girl I'd met. She was engaged to be married; I never got beyond the exquisite tacky wetness of her red lips, and our meetings were unpredictable and brief.

One or two other girls flickered, just as chastely, through my last term at Oxford. Mostly it was dust and heat and boredom. One boring, hot, dusty afternoon I took a stroll in north Oxford. I saw a few people bending over a motionless form on the pavement. It was a girl, covered to the neck by a red coat. There had been an accident. The scene disturbed and excited me. I went back to my room and wrote a poem. As I wrote it, I felt a prickly sensation at my nape. I knew suddenly I wanted to be a poet, more than anything else. I wrote another, about a cinema usherette. I showed them to John Bayley. He thought they showed promise, predicting that I'd be a late developer.

The last few weeks of term were dragging terribly. I had an impulse to go home for a few days. I made the excuse that my wife had pneumonia. My landlady was full of concern, having met her on her summer visit and found her terribly sweet. She brought me a little get-well present for her, tastefully packaged. Curiosity made me rip off the string and paper, which I carelessly dropped into my waste basket. I stuffed the scented soaps into my suitcase.

On returning from my 'sick leave', I told her my wife was better; but found her unresponsive, curt. I was taken aback. The obvious reason didn't occur to me for some time. How stupid not to realise she would have found the wrapping paper.

It was on this return journey, overnight, that my travelling companion put her head out of the window at Reading and said, "I wish you were coming with me!"

FIVE

Dream Books

I was at Paddington, sometime in the mid-evening. I needed to get to Wokingham, but when I asked for a ticket at the desk the girl said the last train had gone. She had to get to Wokingham too, so perhaps we could share a taxi? I agreed. Then we were strolling along New College Lane, in Oxford. She was an artist, the girl told me; and she loved literature. Hardy was her favourite writer. She asked me what I did, and I said I was writing a thesis on the problems of translating Pushkin into English, but really I was a poet. We walked on, talking pleasantly; I thought, What an interesting girl! I was lucky to meet her like that. We could become friends.

As I drifted awake, the dream was still vivid in my mind. I had rarely had such a clear dream. I lay in my house in Hereford, on a Sunday morning in autumn, thinking about the dream. It expressed a desire that I might meet someone in Oxford where, in my mid-life sabbatical, I was spending four days of each week. After three weeks I hadn't made any friends, and felt lonely there. Also present in the dream, perhaps, was my eternal wish to bring the fragments of my life into unity. The vision had been so lifelike that I ought to be feeling disappointed; but it brought me a peculiar happiness and sense of lightness.

My wife and children appeared to be still asleep. In my dressing-gown I went to the kitchen to make myself tea and toast. I fed the cats. I took my breakfast tray and *The Sunday Times* to bed. I lay in late, as usual, while the house gradually came to life: the bathroom-door slamming, pop music playing, curtains being drawn, dishes being rattled. I dressed in time for dinner. Sunday dinner had long been the family ritual of the week, the one occasion when all four of us would be together, talking. There was often an embarrassed silence, which I would try to break by cracking a joke. 'Dad's Sunday joke' had become a joke in itself.

In the afternoon I worked in my study; watched television at teatime, a tray on my lap before the fire. Then, as always, I said "Cheerio", got into my car and drove to Denise's house. She was getting Ross ready for bed. I read and watched TV again. At ten-thirty I said "Cheerio" and drove home. As far as the weekends were concerned, the pattern of my life hadn't changed.

But on Monday morning I packed my hold-all, Maureen stocked me up with Cornish pasties, and drove me to the station. It wasn't unlike saying cheerio to my mother as a National Serviceman or undergraduate. My tiny functional cell in New College's graduate hall of residence was just as grimy with food stains as had been the gracious room I'd shared with Bill. I chain-smoked now, and there was sliced bread; but I was no tidier nor wiser. That evening I met Andrew, my friend from Hertford College, and his new girlfriend for a drink. He was finding his course at the Department of Education more interesting than I'd found my Dip.Ed. course in those far-off days; and he couldn't stop winding his body around his girlfriend. They were sharing a tiny flat in a large postgraduate hostel. I was jealous of his happiness. They left early.

Strolling back through the garden quad, I half expected to see Bill's monkish phantom, but saw only a few absurdly schoolboyish undergrads.

My short Oxford week had fallen into a routine. I worked in the Bodleian, reading appallingly dated translations of Pushkin. I attended two obligatory though, for me, useless classes in Bibliography and Palaeography. In the latter, each of us in turn had to translate an indecipherable Elizabethan script into modern English. The young students were razor-sharp; I was incompetent. The tutor, though, indulged me because of my age.

At the end of that session, on Thursday morning, I would normally have rushed back to my room, grabbed my hold-all, and headed for the station. Today I took it at a slower pace, since I had an early-evening engagement with my publishers in London. I found myself at Paddington around nine o'clock, in time for the last train to Hereford. I watched the big departures board flicker up destinations. One column ended at Hereford; another, at Penzance. As always at this terminus, I felt tension and sadness. Cornwall was alien, yet home; Hereford was home, yet alien. Or vice versa. If I took the night train, as so often in the past, my father wouldn't be waiting at Redruth.

The Hereford column flashed the platform number, and I joined the surge forward. Boarding a smoking compartment, I spotted empty seats opposite two young women. I stowed my hold-all and sat down. I observed the young women.

From their accent they were American and I guessed they were students; one was brown-haired and plump, the other was slim and had blonde hair cut very short and stubbly. Her manner was as jagged as her hair; she smoked with nervous, jerky movements. The more sedate brunette was quoting from the paperback at which they were both glancing; I saw it was a dream book. Some of the phoney, often sexual, interpretations in the book were amusing and I found myself drawn in to their gaiety. Our shared amusement broke down the barriers. The train drew out. The brunette rested her head, closed her eyes and dozed. Her friend and I chatted.

"What do you do?" I asked.

"I'm a student at the Ruskin College of Art in Oxford."

"Oh!" I said. "I'm at Oxford too." I explained my middle-aged sabbatical. "I'm writing a thesis on the problems of translating Pushkin." I added, striving to impress, "But really I'm a poet."

"I write poetry too."

"Really?"

"Uh-huh."

"Who's your favourite poet?"

"Yeats."

We chatted on. Conscious that I was twice her age, I tentatively suggested we meet for a drink on Monday. She agreed. The train was drawing into Swindon, where they had to change for Oxford, and she nudged her friend awake.

When the train was chugging on again through darkened countryside, I congratulated myself on my lucky break. Ten minutes elapsed before the memory of my weekend dream sprang into my mind. Paddington in mid-evening . . . Oxford . . . Pushkin . . . an artistic girl . . . It was unbelievable: the meeting and our conversation had followed the dream almost exactly. Yeats instead of Hardy, that was all—both favourites of mine.

Most uncanny of all, they had been reading a dream book.

I took the predictive dream as a good omen. I saw Amanda, the American, two or three times a week, and no longer felt lonely from Mondays to Thursdays.

I was soon going to be off to America myself, having arranged a short reading tour. On one of my weekends at home I called in at a bookshop to find some reading matter for the long flights. A paperback of Kuznetsov's *Babi Yar* caught my eye. Its very length appealed to me, though normally I run a mile from long novels. Anyway, there was nothing else I wanted to read. At my rate of reading novels, this would keep me going for the two weeks of my trip.

Before stowing the book away, to await my flight like a virgin, I glanced through it, hovering on the chapter in which Kuznetsov related the Babi Yar genocide. Mostly he used an eye-witness account, by the only victim who had escaped from the first-day massacre. Her account moved me deeply.

I returned to Bibliography, Palaeography and Pushkin. But one afternoon, as I was sitting doing nothing in my cell, Babi Yar came back to me, and linked up with the wild monologue, *The Woman to Sigmund Freud*, rotting in a drawer at home. There were extraordinary connections. My anonymous heroine had also made a terrified escape from an unspecified danger. I had based her fantasy on the elements: water, fire, earth and air. The lake had flooded, the hotel burned, mourners had been buried in an avalanche, skiers had fallen through the air to their deaths. All these events were echoed at

Babi Yar: the victims had fallen into the ravine; Dina Pronicheva, the survivor, had been terrified of being buried alive as earth was flung down on the sea of bodies; later, the Nazis had burned the dug-up corpses, trying to hide their crime; then, under the Soviets, a dam had burst, flooding the ravine and most of Kiev.

I couldn't escape the conviction that the woman of my poem was Dina Pronicheva—or someone very like her.

At that point I began to see deeper thematic connections, both through similarity and contrast. Freud, like most of the early psychoanalysts, had been Jewish. So were most of their patients. One could interpret the psychoanalytical movement as in part a Jewish response to anti-semitism. The most 'fashionable' problem dealt with was hysteria; mythologically, hysteria was associated with powers of premonition —the Delphic oracle and Cassandra. Might not some of the hysterias treated by Freud have been caused by apprehensions of the future rather than suppressions of the past?

The terrors suffered by Freud's patients were pathetic metaphors of the *real* hallucinations of an event such as Babi Yar. Freud strove compassionately and over months to lay bare one person's psyche and erotic personality; the Nazis got thirty thousand people to undress, in a single day—quite without Freudian prurience—then shot them.

The white hotel, life, was made for pleasure and happiness; but there was something in its very fabric which demanded self destruction.

These connections occurred to me, mistily, in the space of a minute or two, and left me shaking with excitement. I now knew that *The Woman to Sigmund Freud* was the start of a novel which would end at Babi Yar. Eros and thanatos. It couldn't be called anything but *The White Hotel*.

I spent the rest of the obsessional day planning the general scheme of the book. The main problem or challenge would be stylistic: how to move from the tumultuous and jagged couplets of the poem to the sober, detailed prose which would be necessary for the Babi Yar section? The centrepiece, I decided, would be a case history in the style of Freud; I had long wanted to write a novella imitating his lucid and poetic narratives. The end of the First World War—the seed of Nazism—seemed the right time for my heroine's analysis. In order to construct that heroine, I would need much more material that she had 'written'. I would 'ask' her to write, using the third person, an erotic fantasy in prose based on her verses. I would create the narrative as intuitively, as unconsciously, as possible; then decide what kind of woman, with what personal history, might conceivably have had such fantasies. I knew only that she should be roughly the same age as the century. In the event, she was born ten years earlier.

Following Freud's analysis, I would have to move her fairly swiftly from 1919 to 1941. The style would be realistic and impersonal, but also lyrical in parts: so leading to, yet contrasting with, the grim slow-moving realism of Babi Yar.

By midnight, all that remained was to write the novel. I couldn't wait to begin. I leapt, next morning, straight from bed to the typewriter. But first I had to write to various institutions in America cancelling my readings, pleading illness.

Nearly all my American trips have been botched, in one way or another. There was the Spring of '67, when I persuaded my College to let me take up a Fellowship in Writing at a minor University in St Paul, Minnesota. It was a young and unknown University, so could only afford a young and unknown British poet. From an early spring in England I flew to frozen, snowdrifted streets. I was lonely, homesick and domestically incompetent in my isolated campus apartment. I wrote homesick, lovesick letters to Maureen, taking her completely by surprise. Recuperating from a hysterectomy, she and the children were in Cornwall with relatives. They would visit the only family in the village with a phone to receive my anguished calls. I also started to smoke seriously, since cigarettes were cheap.

Then I fell in with a tall, Nordic-looking student. Making love she froze, like the icicles at the window, at the point of orgasm. It wasn't a comfortable experience. Anyway, I saw the Minnesota semester as providing a fresh, pure rebirth in my tangled life. I was determined to keep it simple, despite this inauspicious start. A few days later, the Dean of Studies invited me to his office. Crewcut and freshfaced, as befitted a Methodist College bureaucrat, he affably congratulated me on my first lecture. His wife, he said, had told him it was wonderful. Just as I was relaxing, his tone changed: "Mr Thomas, it's my information that you have started an affair with one of our students. Is it true?"

Shakily I denied it. I couldn't see how he could have found out; but he seemed confident of the facts. Having been lectured on proper behaviour, I staggered away. Ingrid, when I told her, was upset. I said we'd have to cool it. In a way, I felt relieved.

Her best friend, a honey-blonde, told me Ingrid was receiving psychological counselling from the Dean of Women. The disturbed girl had gone straight from my bed and spilled the beans—foolishly assuming it would be confidential.

The tiny scandal subsided; the snows melted to an arid brown heat, without intervening Spring. I played over and over on a borrowed gramophone Delius' *On Hearing the First Cuckoo in Spring*, and Elgar, and for the first and only time in my life longed for the fresh, dewy green of Herefordshire. But my homesick torment was drawing to a close; it seemed safe, when Ingrid proposed it, to resume our short-lived affair. She promised not to tell the Dean of Women. We made love again, and again she froze on me. She had been raped at fifteen.

At that point, unfortunately though joyously, I fell in love with her best friend, the honey-blonde, and she with me. She was fresh and beautiful, and my stomach caved every time she approached. I didn't want the semester to end.

I was sitting alone under a shady tree one day when I saw the Dean of Studies. He veered towards me; my heart sank. We hadn't collided since the ticking-off in his office. Greeting me pleasantly, he sat beside me.

"It sure is hot today!"

"Yes."

His voice became lamentful. "Mr Thomas, I hear that you've been sleeping with *another* of our students."

I croaked a denial. Lynette and I were friendly, that was all. I didn't know many people here; it got lonely.

"Well, maybe that's our fault. I'll see about fixing up a little gathering. But my information is that she's been seen leaving your apartment in the morning, with a suitcase."

I denied it, truthfully. She had never stayed overnight. The girls at the sorority next door must have been giving vent to their imaginations.

"I've talked to Lynette, and told her you're a happily married man."

I didn't know how to reply to that. He said, "I've heard nothing but good about your *work*," with an emphasis that implied that, so far as my character was concerned, he had heard nothing but bad. He stood up and walked away over the scant, burnt grass.

Lynette went into hiding. I visited her once at a motel, and made love to her with an anguished passion. Ingrid, she said, had been desperately jealous and told everyone. My aspirations towards a simple, pure interlude had turned into complexity and opprobrium. Lovesick for Lynette, I flew home.

The epoch of miniskirts had dawned during my absence. When my students crossed their legs you could see their briefs; but I mourned the more discreet eroticism of a flashed stocking top. The yards of boring nylon they now wore seemed as arid as Minnesota's grass.

SIX

The Nightmare of History

Turning poetic metaphors into literal fact—so that hair actually caught fire—I plunged into my patient's prose fantasy. I was prepared, of course, to revise the original poem, if the novel demanded it; but in fact nothing had to be changed. I added, late on, one inessential couplet.

The prose fantasy wrote itself easily and swiftly, in two typefaces, one in Oxford and one at home. The novel consumed me. Whether I was eating, drinking, or sleeping, alone or companioned, my mind was running on what would happen next. Novels play havoc with relationships—even more than poems, since there are breaks between poems. The irony was that I'd come to Oxford intending to make up for my misspent youth by having a bloody good time; yet here I was, working not eight hours a day but sixteen! I was forced to accept I was a workaholic.

It put stress on my fragile friendship with Amanda. Her intensity, expressed in fierce glances and jagged smoking, was too much; she hardly ever slept, and at eleven her evening had just begun, whereas I would be choked up with unwritten images or ideas and craved my typewriter. She insisted that I stay; I grew weary of walking back to college at 3 a.m., through snow and ice—it was a bad winter. Also she was urging me to spend the odd weekend in Oxford, which I had no intention of doing.

The vivid and joyous dream of meeting a girl at Paddington, and its coming true, now seemed to me to be a single epiphany pointing towards the novel, in which a young woman on a train—the travelling psyche—is a dominant image. My novel, like the epiphany, blended dream and reality. The girl I had met sold tickets for a journey, she made it possible.

And our destination, via Oxford, was Wokingham, which suggested awakening.

Not needing Amanda any more, I broke with her.

I was no longer sorry that Andrew didn't need much of my company. We still met usually once a week at the Turf Tavern, and talked about our dismal prospects for a congenial job at the end of the year. He confessed to me, rather slyly when his girlfriend wasn't listening, that he was writing a journal; it was being typed by a girl who was too stupid to understand it—fortunately. He barked a laugh. His divorce having come through, he married his beautiful and vivacious student. They seemed happy; yet I noticed, with some pleasure, that the improvements she had wrought in him weren't lasting; his clothes were returning to their normal grubby state, he was drinking more heavily and engaging in drunken quarrels. I hadn't liked him so much without his *angst*. Now he was becoming more like his old disreputable self and I was glad. He was again Onegin.

Indeed, he might easily be, I thought, one of those surly, handsome, demonic Pushkinian heroes. He would devour his young wife with kisses, then for no reason fling her aside. I watched him pick a jealous fight with a student-poet, then, filled with remorse, offer him two tickets for a May Ball.

Finding I had loaned, and never received back, my only copy of my first pamphlet of poems, *Personal and Possessive*, he goodnaturedly stole a copy from a friend and gave it to me. Yes, a true Pushkin hero.

So far as my academic Pushkin was concerned, I decided to call a halt. I had written eight thousand words towards the thesis: enough to submit at the end of year assessment. I thought I would probably abandon the half-hearted B.Litt. at that stage, since if I chose to do the second year I would have to pay my own fees. Nor would a B.Litt. be of much use; with the cut-backs, those Colleges of Education that remained open were desperately trying to turn themselves into fourth-rate Universities by grabbing people with doctorates, however dull or inexperienced. I had tried the nearest College, Worcester, and not even been interviewed. I had the impression that if

Shakespeare applied for a Drama post he wouldn't stand a chance.

Failing a miracle, I would try to be made redundant. I was hopeful of *The White Hotel*. I thought it could become the best thing I'd written, and might pay the mortgage for a year or two.

The prose-fantasy had been dream-written almost; with the Freudian analysis I would have to apply concentrated logical thought. And I knew next to nothing about Freudian theory; what fascinated me about him was his myth-making power, his capacity to find a mythic grandeur in the psyche, just at the time when other sciences had been reducing man's stature. But my appreciation of the poet in Freud wouldn't be enough to create a convincing analysis.

I plunged into a reading of Freud. New College library had his collected works. I analysed his analyses; in particular the case of Fräulein Elisabeth von R., since it seemed to be about the right length and had an artistically satisfying form. Gradually two aspects of the case histories impressed themselves on me. First, they followed the classical structure of Greek drama: ignorance suddenly and painfully banished by a blinding flash of light. I wondered if the discoverer of the Oedipus complex hadn't sometimes imposed his own aesthetically pleasing resolution. Secondly, these studies were Viennese seduction stories. A troubled young woman came in and lay down on a couch; Freud, his cigar flaring, got to work on her, striving to strip her naked. Day after day the struggle went on, behind locked doors. Her powerful resistance made it all the more exciting. At long last, and quite unexpectedly, he broke through, drawing blood from the hymen. She writhed, panted, fought, but he went inexorably on. After-wards, bruised, weeping, she talked it over with him. He began to lose interest. There would be a friendly but rueful goodbye. He might meet her by chance years later, while on holiday at Gastein, say; they would exchange a few awkward phrases, like any pair who had once, long ago, been lovers.

I set out to echo Freud's style—which came fairly easily —and to imitate his form, which was hard. But first I had to 'find the woman'. I still had no idea who she was. The most important pages of the novel were the first half-dozen of *Frau Anna G.*, in which Freud recounts her life story. It would be pointed out to me that Anna and Lisa (her real name) make —almost—analysis; and that Gē is the Greek earth-mother. Anyway—at last I knew something about my heroine; but what would Freud make of her hysteria? For the answer I looked in her fantasy writings and, I suppose, in my unconscious.

As much as anything, Freud's voice, dry, remorseless and subtly erotic, carried me through. If the voice rang true, the chances were that I wasn't going too far astray, I hoped. I'd cover my ignorance by writing a note to the effect that it was a literary composition with no pretensions to genuine analysis. I enjoyed imitating his voice; it gave me constraints, such as I was accustomed to in poetry and which a novel lacks. I don't think I have a prose style that is my own. As I turned to the third-person narrative of the next section, *The Health Resort*, I had to look for an appropriate style. I imagined a contemporary Turgenev, and translated it from his non-existent Russian.

I kept discovering new things about Lisa Erdman. Much that was in her letters to Freud took me by surprise. I was very fond of her—and soon I was going to submit her to a terrible death. I had to screw myself up to the Babi Yar episode, both because of its unbearable subject matter and because painfully detailed description doesn't come naturally to me.

There were special problems, stemming from my need to draw extensively from Dina Pronicheva's testimony. I had no doubt it was necessary, for several reasons. My unique character, Lisa, was now becoming a part of history, part of the amorphous mass of victims. So I wanted the events to be authentic. It would have seemed immoral had I, a comfortable Briton, fictionalised the holocaust.

Moreover, the book had sprung from the emotional impact which Dina's testimony had made on me. I identified her intimately with Lisa. In my imagination she *was* Lisa; or at least her very close shadow.

Finally, the plot demanded that Lisa be an observer of the Babi Yar massacre, before becoming another victim. She had to be one of the last group to die, in order that the Nazis and Ukrainians, treading among the corpses, would provide an 'alternative' explanation for her hysteria. That meant she and her stepson must have been spared temporarily, ordered to sit on the hillock where the real Dina Pronicheva sat. She would have observed the same events.

I decided, for these reasons, that for the objective details I would rely on Dina's account. I would permeate it with the imagined thoughts and feelings of Lisa and her stepson.

Obviously I would make a formal acknowledgement of my indebtedness. But that didn't seem enough; I wanted to suggest the symbiosis of Dina and Lisa in the text itself. It wasn't easy without being heavy handed; but I arrived at a way of doing it. I had referred to Dina as an actress whom Lisa recognised among the victims. Then, when Lisa is lying in the ravine, she dreams of waiting until dark, finding her son, and escaping up the ravine side. After a description of night falling and the bodies settling, I wrote:

> A woman *did* scramble up the ravine side, after dark. It was Dina Pronicheva. And when she grasped hold of a bush to pull herself over, she *did* come face to face with a boy, clothed in vest and pants, who also had inched his way up. He scared Dina with his whisper: "Don't be scared, lady! I'm alive too."
>
> Lisa had once dreamt those words, when she was taking the thermal springs at Gastein with Aunt Magda. But it is not really surprising, for she had clairvoyant gifts and naturally a part of her went on living with these survivors; Dina, and the little boy who trembled and shivered all over.
>
> Dina survived to be the only witness, the sole authority for what Lisa saw and felt. Yet it had happened thirty thousand times; always in the same way and always differently. Nor can the living ever speak for the dead.

As I was writing what I had intended to be the last section, I began strongly to feel it couldn't end there, with thirty thousand corpses in a ravine. My novel wasn't about the holocaust, but about the journey of the soul, which I believe is endless. I needed a spiritual fantasy—in the sense of Dante's 'high fantasy'—to succeed Lisa's sexual fantasy and Freud's intellectual fantasy.

A sentence in Dina's account gave me a clue. The rumour, she said, was that they were to be sent off to Palestine. Lisa was Catholic; I had deliberately played down her Jewishness—indeed, she may not have any Jewish blood in her at all. She would know about Purgatory. It would be natural for her to imagine that existence in terms of the Holy Land. That is, if she does imagine it and it is not real. I wanted both to be possible.

I tried to mix realistic, down-to-earth images, of sand and dust and refugee huts, with lyrical passages: *I am the rose of Sharon.* . . Above all I tried to convey that it was a place where people still suffered, but the suffering was redemptive. As Lisa met her long-dead mother, her face scarred from a hotel fire, I thought of the final, anguished lines of Yeats's *Purgatory*:

> O God,
> Release my mother's soul from its dream!
> Mankind can do no more. Appease
> The misery of the living and the remorse of the dead.

Reading through the typescript, I realised I would have to do a lot of revision, but essentially it was all right. For the first time I thought of its readers: it was asking a lot of them to plunge them straight into an erotic poem. I could lead into it through some letters, from and to Freud. For the opening letter I chose to relate, from Ferenczi's viewpoint, Freud's triumphant voyage to America in 1909, bringing the enlightenment of psychoanalysis to the new world. The dark places of the psyche were being illuminated and thereby exorcised. Who could have imagined the holocaust? Yet some of the events of that journey seemed premonitory: notably Freud's fainting fit when Jung, the Aryan, described the excavation of peat-bog corpses in North Germany. The form of *The White Hotel* struck me as musical, and the opening letter was a kind of overture.

I interrupted my writing to sit end-of-year papers in Bibliography and Palaeography. The piece of Elizabethan calligraphy we had to translate had me floundering. Once more there was a Viva: three examiners, a dapper young man and two severe ladies, instead of twenty. One of the female dons started by saying I had passed the written tests: the tutors sent their congratulations. Instantly the dapper young man said, "That's good; because it shows us Mr Thomas is capable of scholarly work. I was not convinced of it by the Pushkin essay. It seemed to me rather superficial and to lack documentation."

It was fair criticism. I recalled Pushkin's official report on a plague of locusts in the Chersonese:

> The locusts were flying, flying,
> Then they came to earth,
> They crawled, they ate up everything,
> And then flew off again.

I put on a suit for dinner that evening. An elderly tutor from my undergraduate days had discovered I was in the College —the first time anyone had noticed my presence—and invited me to High Table. As I was getting ready, Andrew and his wife burst in. He too was smartly dressed; they were going out for a drink, and wondered if I'd like to come. I made my apologies. While he was in the bathroom having a pee, his wife whispered that she was very worried about their marriage; he was drinking heavily. She was going home for the weekend to have a break; could she perhaps ring me and have a chat? I nodded, Andrew came out, and they left.

That Saturday I was in Hereford as usual. The post came. A package in Andrew's elegant handwriting. Puzzled, I tore off the brown paper wrappings. A weighty book, bound in stiff plain black. I opened it. Single-space typing. Oh Lord, his journal! He wanted me to offer an opinion, it would seem. How embarrassing! But why hadn't he brought it with him on Wednesday? After the type there were several handwritten pages—diary entries, I saw, from the last couple of weeks —then blanks. I read the last entry. "I have nothing more to say. It has been stated already. I depart quietly to that region to which I truly belong."

My God, suicide! I rushed to the phone, dialled his ex-wife. She was bright; sobered at my agitation. Her post had just come: she went to get it. When she came back she was sobbing. She would ring the Oxford police.

I was pacing around demented, strangely excited, when the phone rang. So quickly? But it was his new wife, I didn't want to alarm her, perhaps unnecessarily. We had an unreal conversation about how to rescue the marriage. I felt deeply sorry for her: so young, and trying so hard.

I ended it as quickly as I could. The phone rang again. A ghastly voice: "He's dead."

I collapsed in a torrent of sobs. I loved him. We had all loved him, but he couldn't love himself.

The following week another journal was sent to me. It was from Lois, my sister, and was in red flexible binding. She was alone in California, but eternally hopeful: "Everything that happens in life is okay." All shall be well and all manner of thing shall be well.

"But why am I still churned up about it, eight years later?" I demand. "Why do I still miss him? Why am I still angry with him for dying?"

"I think," she says, "he is connected with your father in some way."

I lie considering this. It's absurd. Andrew was younger than I; a highbrow, an intellectual. Nothing like my father.

Cornwall and Armenia

Earliest memories.

I am being held lightly, weightlessly, in my mother's arms. I know it's my mother even though I can't see her. What has shocked me awake, into consciousness, is a choking, hacking cough. It is the back parlour at St Martin's Villa; dark except for a haze of light from the window and the face of an aunt peering at me. Her face is level with mine; she is pale and worried. I think she is Auntie Nellie. At six weeks, I've been told, I had whooping cough. God knows how I recognise worry at six weeks old, but I do.

A table is laid outside the front door. A birthday cake with one candle. I have to blow out the flame. I don't want to, I am playing my mother up. It's recorded in a snapshot. It must have been an unusually warm January day.

I am being carried into the front sittingroom, which is dim. A withered crone in a bed reaches for me, and I shrink away. My grandmother offers me a bunch of green grapes, and I take them. She died before I was two.

I am being propelled in a pushchair up a road. A bungalow is being built. My father stands in his white overalls, smiling at us, amid half-built walls of concrete blocks. I'm aware of sky above him.

The first sight of my mother. I have been sick for weeks with kidney trouble. The doctor says I can have a little fish. My mother sits by my bed and offers me a cup of milk. I draw back; she cajoles me; I gag the foul milk into her surprised lap.

She is pulling up her dress, sitting on the toilet. There's something funny about between-her-legs.

Our front room: wireless, piano and stool, three-piece suite, redcoated wooden negro holding an ashtray. I am sitting on

a pouffe, listening to my father talking to a couple who
have called. Mother is in the kitchen preparing some supper.
The talk disturbs me, they are grave. Unnoticed by them a
huge, skinny-legged spider crosses the carpet. I jump up and
scamper to meet it, cover it, peel it from my sandal, then sit
down again quietly. Later, I am standing with my father
waving goodbye to our visitors. We linger in the porch.
Gazing up at a night of brilliant stars, never noticed before, I
say, "Daddy, is it peace or war?" He replies, "Peace." I feel
reassured. We go in.

I stand to attention outside Mona's cottage at Restronguet,
facing the camera with the estuary behind it. I wear a helmet
and carry a gun on my shoulder. I smile proudly, but the
sunlight blinds me and I squint just as the camera clicks. My
eyes are squeezed shut in the snap.

I am crying in a classroom, unable to let go of my mother's
hand. I sniffle most of the day, which goes on for ever.

I am scolded by my teacher for not being able to tie up my
shoes. The rubber stench of a gas mask. The urine odour of
raincoats; my weak, stupid feeling in the presence of a girl with
short straight blonde hair; her mother and mine laughing
because I like her.

Sickness. I'm scolded because when I go to the blackboard
I've no idea what to write with the piece of chalk. I sit, deeply
ashamed.

Men in white coats placing foul-smelling black rubber over
my mouth; I gag into oblivion. When I wake up in bed, my
mother is beside me. It's natural that my throat is sore and I feel
sick. She picks up *Gulliver's Travels* and reads to me. I am
soothed by hearing again how the Lilliputians staked Gulliver
to the ground.

I am picked out by Miss Dyer the headmistress to join
her special group for reading. We reach a word no one
knows, but I guess 'laughter'; she says, "Good boy!" and I
laugh.

A picnic with Donald Craze and his mother on Carn Marth.
He and I stand on a granite rock gazing at the dark tarn. Then,
on a grassy spot, my playmate chases me round our mothers,

crying "Shimmy-shirty! Shimmy-shirty!" I trip over Mother's picnic basket. Agony. They carry me down the path; a quarryman looks at my arm. "I think it's broken." Hospital; the rubber mask. Pain. Elbow not set properly. Have to go to Truro Infirmary. Nurse gives me a cup of milk. That horrible taste. I hide the milk skins under my pillow. Cry because I've been left. About to go home, after two weeks, when an infectious patient is brought in. The ward isolated. Can't understand why my parents don't come anymore. Once, twice, I see their faces pressed to the window; they have climbed up the fire-escape. They can't bear seeing my tears, don't come again. At last, a birthday party for one of the children. Jam sandwiches. I don't like bread-and-butter-and-jam, but I like the jam sandwiches. I can go home. Back at 'Beverly', I ask for a jam sandwich. "I don't want bread-and-butter-and-jam I want a jam sandwich." I carry a seaside bucket filled with sand, to straighten my right arm.

Durgan, by the Helford; a flash of pebbles and water.

Andrew and I had found different answers to our similar problems. I needed to argue with him about his suicide. I wrote him a letter, in the form of a poem, in which I said I forgave him but would never understand. It wasn't true; I would come to understand.

The women in his life were, of course, devastated. Two years afterwards, I bumped into his first wife in Hereford; she looked pale and shaky. She told me she had just met an old Hereford student, who had enquired how Andrew was. "I said, Oh, he's fine! I couldn't bring myself to say he was dead." I could understand that.

With Oxford and that death behind me, I settled painfully to the life of a writer. I feared the change would damage my art. For twenty years, the Muse had been a mistress, the more loved because my times with her were stolen. Now she would become my wife. I wasn't sure how I would cope.

The change also made it more likely that I would write novels. Poems come in fits and starts; whereas I would need to be continuously absorbed. And I would need my wife the Muse to earn us money.

My actual wife, or rather ex-wife, was as loyal and supportive as she had always been in backing my decision to take the risk. But the strains from our peculiar half-life together didn't grow less severe. Caitlin left home to go to College. We missed her, and the house seemed more silent.

The view of rough lawn and trees through the french windows of my study became oppressive. Walking to the shops for cigarettes, I felt that my mind wasn't quite in my skull. My tendency to introspection and reserve was encouraged now that the main outlet for sociability, the College, was dead. As the leaves reddened, I desperately mourned the chat, gossip, jokes and banter, as well as the sense of having a framework to my life.

At least the early response to *The White Hotel* typescript was encouraging; especially in the United States, where Viking Press had taken it. I received long letters from various editors expressing an enthusiasm that was obviously sincere. On the other hand, Gollancz was having trouble in persuading a paperback firm to publish it. Picador, who had first refusal, rejected it. My editor there wrote me a kind letter of explanation: he found parts of the novel very powerful, but on the whole thought it 'wasn't a patch on' *The Flute-Player*. I replied that if it was half as good as Viking thought, and twice as good as he thought, it should do quite well. Then Penguin turned it down, on the grounds that it wasn't commercial.

I was more concerned with the sheet in my typewriter, which stayed depressingly blank. Pushkin haunted me—I continued making some translations. I kept thinking of the last words of *Autumn*: "It sails. Where shall we sail?" I loved the way he would break off abruptly, as if to say, That's it! I'm bored! It's enough!

Where would I sail? I had no idea.

Another broken-off work by Pushkin began to obsess me: *Egyptian Nights*. A comfortable Petersburg poet is disturbed in his study by the unannounced arrival of a scruffy Italian *improvisatore* who asks for his help. The fragmentary story moves from prose to verse, from the present to the past, from realism—tinged with the uncanny—to myth: for the Italian improvises in public on the theme of 'Cleopatra and her Lovers', the queen's challenge to her courtiers to accept death at dawn in exchange for a night of passion. Eros and thanatos again.

I dreamed of continuing his story, in some way. I liked the blurring of boundaries, in form and atmosphere. I couldn't write a straight novel; but I couldn't write a straight poem any more either.

I would improvise.

Chance and a *Times Literary Supplement* editor took a hand. I was asked if I would review several books of translation. Among them was an *Anthology of Armenian Poetry*, edited and translated by Diana Der Hovanessian and Marzbed Margossian. I was overwhelmed by the book. I knew nothing about Armenia; it was news to me that two million Armenians had been killed by Turks in 1915. The ancient country was kept alive by faith and by its language—a language distilled by great and heroic poets.

My depression and my petty problems were put in perspective by the tragedy and grandeur of the Armenians. The genocide would have to find a place in my improvisation. "Why are you obsessed with violence?" is a question I'm often asked. A holocaust in *The White Hotel*, and then another one! But that's the story of the twentieth century.

I wrote to Diana Der Hovanessian, the main translator, the first fan-letter of my life. Pleased with my *TLS* review, she wrote back from Boston. Since I was planning to make up for my aborted tour of the previous year, she offered to find me a couple of readings in her area. I wanted to know more about Armenia.

A few weeks before my departure I was struck down by a mysterious illness. Days and nights I tossed in high fever. It was clearly a punishment for having lied about being ill when cancelling the earlier tour.

The fever passed; I was still shaky and unwell, but decided to go ahead. By now I was into a confused improvisation: a voyage . . . a Russian poet . . . fever . . . Cleopatra . . . a transatlantic flight . . . I was making my own flight even as I was planning Surkov's flight. Superstition gripped me: what if we crashed? Was it healthy mixing up life and art in this way? Might not the Fates punish me for it? This was truly the madness of art. But I no longer found it possible to stand back from my life when writing.

Russia is a convenience for western writers. If Dante were alive today he wouldn't have to invent Hell. I envied Soviet poets their shortage of accommodation, sometimes making a *ménage à trois* unavoidable and conventional.

I flew to Boston, and Diana met me. We were already friends through our letters. She cooked us a beautiful dinner at her home in Cambridge, and we chatted about my tour. In the night my sickness returned. I staggered to her bedroom, woke her up, and said, "I'm afraid I'll have to go home tomorrow." She was very kind and understanding. When I got home I was given a kidney x-ray and found I had a stone blocking a ureter. I remained sickly till Christmas, then the stone passed through.

Surkov also stays with an Armenian artist, and feels ill, but there the similarities end. He flew on to Arizona to have an affair with an English schoolgirl. Surkov is a bastard.

Childhood and Cats

War brought with him his camp follower, Love. Once the fear of invasion had passed—at five years old, it meant little to me—I was caught up in my sister's intense romantic excitement. Our sleepy town was invaded nightly by Battle of Britain airmen; later, by Yanks from D-Day training camps. Their advance parties came just as Lois, vivacious, freckled, redheaded, was leaving school; it almost seemed as if Hitler had consulted her. She rushed home from her office job, ate her tea standing, changed her clothes and refreshed her make-up on the run. A different guy brought her home from the dance or cinema every night.

It's strange how she affected me so much, for she never took the slightest notice of me, nor I of her on the more mundane level. She was a vivid flame, warming the house more than the Cornish range or the coal fire. When I recall the slender searchlights interweaving in the black sky, I think of her frantic dressings; when I recall the midnight glow on the horizon as the oil dumps of Swan Pool burned, I think of the auburn hair she inherited from my father. I can never see passionate embraces in the London blitz, in some film, without remembering, in a strange vicarious way, the press of my sister's lips against the mouth of some airman perhaps only nights away from death.

I'm sure my father felt the glamour of it too. Her bedroom door open, he would try to press clumsy kisses on her, and she would push him away, protesting; while my mother, from the kitchen, scolded her for not being affectionate.

The boys in blue, and later the jaunty GIs, never got very far with her, I'm sure. No further than the Hollywood heroes in the films she devoured. Walter Pidgeon had once patted her on the head when Father, a studio workman, brought along his baby daughter.

Eighteen when the First World War ended, thirty-nine when the Second began, too young or too old, Father was lucky in war. I think he was lucky in love too; though there may have been moments when he doubted it. I am sure he had strong passions; my mother said as much, after his death; and said that she wasn't so keen on sex. Like mother like daughter, Lois would admit with a chuckle that really she preferred a bar of Cadbury's.

But she loved the romance, the glamour, the chase and escape. At least, that's how it struck my childish senses. My life seemed in comparison uneventful. Mother wouldn't let me play rough games. As a result, when she did let me go off and play with an older boy once, I panicked and almost fell to my death in some old mine workings. I could either risk a six-foot drop into a dark hole by jumping, as the other boy did, or go round the side and risk a hundred-foot drop. I chose the latter, since I was frightened of the dark.

I was frightened of the night. After the lights had been turned off in the bungalow, I took to calling out that I could see a ghost standing in the front doorway. My parents knew you couldn't see the front doorway from my tiny bedroom. They grumbled, but always in the end they let me come to their bedroom and Mother would leave their bed for mine. I would snuggle happily against my father's hot tangy skin—skin seems the right word even though he wore pyjamas: I could see his hairy chest—and I would beg him for a story. I recall a story about a voyage to America, lulling me asleep.

Lawrence talks about the bliss of sleeping with one's mother; and that would have been just as blissful, I suppose, but it didn't happen.

He worked very hard; the lines trenched in his gaunt, kind face. He was also in the Home Guard. I don't think he would have held up the storm troopers for long; but he would have died for us.

It was a friendly house; friends were always dropping in of an evening, after our supper round the fire. Mother was in the kitchen making sandwiches for some callers when another man, old and bald, arrived. She took him into the kitchen. Opening the hatch she whispered at us, "It's Harold's cousin Bertie; he's deaf and dumb."

After a moment's silence Father said, "Then what the hell are you whispering for?" Everyone roared with laughter. My father's laugh was famous: four descending notes; repeated at a higher pitch; then still higher. Work-mates would say, "Heard you in the pictures on Saturday, Harold! What 'ee think of it?"

He loved coming home with droll stories of his work-mates. "Mr Prisk called round; he started talking about his life in India. He said you had to be very careful: if the children went out with a nanny for the day you had to make sure the water was boiled. When he had gone, Freddie turned to me and said, 'What a bleddy man, i'n it, Harold? Sendin' his children out with a bleddy goat!'"

And his laughter would ring out.

"I would say there was a lot of fairly low-keyed unhappiness," she murmurs behind my head.

No. No. We were very happy.

"You were never really a part of the family. You were at the periphery. Perhaps your mother didn't altogether want to have you; so she compensated by fussing you. But the guilt in such situations always nags unconsciously."

I roll my tongue over a troublesome tooth. My whole body is out of order, out of sync with my mind.

"Think about it," she continues. "You have a dream of a dream: your fantasies go back to their California episode, long before you were born. Because you think then they were happy." She pauses; I say nothing. "I get a sense of immense loneliness."

Suddenly I feel immensely lonely. My mouth emits a strangled sigh.

"It's very painful; but you must confront your feelings. Otherwise . . ." She leaves the warning in mid-air.

"God! Do I have to hate them?"

A hesitation. "You have used the word."

Thou hast said.

On the drive back, I pull in beside the village school where Ross is a pupil. I'm the only male parent among the patient gatherers. Also I'm the oldest. I could be a grandfather, smoking in my suave BMW. As I see my scruffy son leave the school, dragging a bag and cello case, I feel a tug of tenderness. So small, so vulnerable; a victim of all our changes.

"Well—did you have a good day?"

"All right."

Wondering what else I can say, I drive off. I didn't want another child yet he is very precious to me, like all my children. I have a problem communicating with them, and am eaten up with guilt about it.

From the back-seat: "Hey, Don: can we stop at Fuorboys?"

"Why?"

"To buy a comic."

"Okay."

We fall silent again. Perhaps my shrink is right, and everything in my childhood is contrary to what I remember. I'm willing to believe it, if it will get me better. It's easy enough to recollect my terrible shyness; the absence of any playmates in the house. Which is the true fantasy: mine, or my analyst's? Or are both false, both true? It's too far away for me to tell. When I look at the childhood snaps of me, taken with my father's box camera, I feel both close to that child and distant. He is I, but also someone else—someone for whom I feel immeasurable tenderness and compassion. I see him much as I see Ross, who comes running with his comic.

I started with *Dandy* and *Beano*; but then, one day when I was in bed with tonsillitis, my mother couldn't get them, and bought me *Champion* instead. At first I was disappointed, because it had no picture stories, only solid columns of words; but once I started reading it I became enthralled by the 'Leader of the Lost Commandos' and 'Rockfist Rogan'. My mother placed a weekly order for it.

Since our bungalow sloped away at the back, there was room for a cellar and a garage—in which Father kept the works van he was entitled to use. At first, our shelter during air raid alerts was under the cellar stairs; later we had a Morrison shelter under the kitchen table. We didn't have to use it often. Only one house was destroyed in Redruth, killing a few people. One Allied plane crashed in a field a quarter-mile away; my mother was in the front passage when the plane crashed, and the crump scared her so much she threw herself forward on to her hands and knees, her pink-bloomered bottom in the air. It became a family joke.

If I took to school three books to be sent for our troops, I would get a Corporal's badge; if five, a Sergeant's. Our house had few books. My father took down all his beloved *National Geographics* from the cupboard and gave them to me, sadly. My school kept the magazines, naturally, and made me a Field Marshal. We also had two free tickets for the Gem, but Father and I went to the Regal instead, since he preferred Bette Davis to Tarzan. The Regal let us use the free tickets.

In the autumn of 1986, an author of my acquaintance asked me if I would examine one of his cats, who had developed hysterical symptoms. Previously placid, the cat had recently taken to pissing against any plastic she could find, and viciously attacked the other cats, who in consequence had become terrified of her.

She was an attractive tabby, about three years old. At my first examination, when without warning she raised her quivering tail and pissed against a video set, then leapt at a timid three-legged ginger, I realised that her owner had correctly diagnosed her problem as one of hysteria. From him, from his companion and their young son, but mostly from the cat's own frightened gaze, I learned the following facts about her background:

She had been born, in a small house some two miles distant, in a litter of four females. Of her mother and sisters, no less than of her father, she had no memory. Cared for by a kind mistress and her son, a lover of animals, she enjoyed a pleasant infancy. In the evenings she was often stroked by a visitor

—my authorial acquaintance. Her mistress rather unimagin-
atively gave her the name Tabitha. She purred in the author's
lap as he arranged to take her away to his house, along with a
grey sister whom he named Lucina, after a previous grey cat he
had housed and loved.

There was a good-natured Cairn terrier in the house of her
birth, who soon overcame any jealousy she may have felt over
the intruders. There were two caged budgerigars, and little
fish in a tank, which the tabby kitten began to covet. But she
was well fed, and life was pleasant.

Life was equally pleasant, once she had got over the initial
shock of moving, in the new house. Indeed, there were some
advantages. Whereas her previous mistress had been out at
work all day and was therefore terribly busy at night, her new
mistress spent most of each day cooking, and juicy titbits
fell to Tabitha's avid mouth. Each evening, the woman sat
alone, watching TV, in front of a blazing fire in winter, and
seemed consoled to stroke Tabitha, perched on her warm,
soft, rounded lap. The grey Lucina was no rival; as lithe and
wild as a squirrel, she was usually outside roaming about. And
tiny, old, black, whiskery Thomas, a veteran of the house,
was no match for the sleek and handsome intruder. Tabitha
thrived and grew fat.

She saw little of her master. While she sat in the warm
kitchen, smelling stew boiling or pasties baking, his typewriter clacked distantly. He emerged for meals, which were
served to him on a tray just as the one o'clock and six o'clock
news started. The couple spoke little; but there was an air of
calm, long-familiar routine which suited the tabby. Around
seven-thirty the taciturn master would put on a coat (except in
summer), select a book, and leave the house. Returning three
hours later, he would glance in at the sittingroom where
Tabitha crouched on her mistress's lap, murmur a greeting,
then vanish again. The typewriter clacked.

Changes occurred. Her mistress started going out sometimes in the evenings too, and Tabitha was left alone with
Thomas, curled in separate chairs. The fire dimmed and
cooled. Then she was away for a whole week. Returning, the

woman said something to the master which made him douse
the television with his remote control; he nodded, and an
expression of profound relief crossed his face. He went to her
and kissed her on the cheek.

But later, when Tabitha was sprawled on her mistress's bed,
he came in, crying. Previously she had, now and then, felt
tears fall from her mistress's eyes on to her fur, during their
peaceful evenings; she had never before seen her master cry.
Then they talked for a long time, with loud voices, and she got
no sleep. For many nights after, he would come into the
sittingroom as usual, removing his coat; but instead of leaving
the room at once he sat down, wept and talked. She cried too,
but in a different, angry, less pitiable way. Sometimes the
phone would ring, and she would leap to it, sending Tabitha
flying. Then her voice would be bright, while the master
buried his head in his hands.

There was a time when the master was away, as often
happened; but there was no cooking, only a most disturbing
emptying of cupboards and packing of cases and tea-chests. At
the end of all this frenzied activity, a different man was
carrying out the cases and chests, and her mistress was picking
her up and fondling her tenderly and sadly. Then she was
gone.

The master came back, the same day, and didn't seem to
know what to do in the silent house. He left lights on in empty
rooms, even at night; there was no warmth or smell of
delicious cooking; the typewriter clacked demently into the
cold small hours. Tabitha was frightened and lonely, didn't
know what had happened. The man paced around the house
and the hard, wintry garden; little whiskery Thomas, who
also grew frightened and scraggy, would follow him on her
plodding, splayed-out legs, wanting to be stroked. He stroked
her more than usual, but paid little attention to Tabitha.

One day there was no breakfast food. The hungry cat found
her master tossing on his bed; he struggled downstairs to open
a tin, but didn't get dressed all day. Nor for many days.

He went away. The house was abandoned. An unknown
woman came twice a day to put food down. Then the master

was back, being helped by Tabitha's first, forgotten mistress up to bed. The forgotten little boy was present, with a forgotten, terrifying Cairn terrier, Tabitha's forgotten ill-tempered mother, and her forgotten ginger-furred sister, now limping on three legs. In a second mad upheaval, suitcases came, chests of books, furniture, a tank full of little golden fish, the caged budgies.

She didn't know whether to be pleased to have more warmth and noise and attention, or sorry because there was so much crowding and confusion, not to mention the rivalry of the other animals. It was not so bad at first, while the atmosphere was pleasant and the master spent the days in bed: fed, like the cats, in a rush before his mistress or wife or ex-wife —his Ani—left for work . . .

"Why do you call Denise your 'Annie'?"

"I was thinking of a poem I wrote, based on a Fijian myth."

But as his typewriter started clacking again, and even more as it gradually fell silent and he spent the days staring dully at the TV screen, the fur began to fly, voices were raised in anger. Tabitha tried to hide, but all her favourite places were taken, or were stuffed with books, bed linen, and so on. Like a depressed human being she started to overeat: diving a paw into the fish tank. When a door was left carelessly open, she jumped on to the birdcage and tried to knock it over. She attacked the other cats, out of fear and bewilderment. Naturally this behaviour didn't endear her to her new mistress, kind though she was. Tabitha sensed her coldness, which increased her alienation and misery. She couldn't stand the shoutings and hooverings and scuttlings. It was at this point that she began to piss, anywhere and any time. She was—as one might say—pissed off.

This, then, was the story which the sad green eyes of the unfortunate young cat told me, supported by the testimony of her master and mistress. I knew the narration must conceal more than it revealed; I urged her to be as open as she possibly could with me, as the only hope of finding a cure for her ills, and turning her hysterical misery into ordinary feline content-ment. I saw evidence of hysteria in two of the other cats:

stunted and crippled Perkins, doubtless afraid of Tabitha, stayed upstairs; mostly she haunted the bathroom, waiting for someone to trickle a tap on so that she could drink—though there was a full dish of water in the kitchen. Emily, their mother, haunted window ledges, eternally asking to be let out and then in again. Lucina I did not see: she still rarely came in. Eluding human hands almost all the time, it was said, she would now and again demand inordinate attention, crawling right up to one's chin and staring intently into one's eyes, digging her claws into the skin.

The dog, apparently, was unchanged, goodnatured still. Only old black whiskery Thomas, I was assured, had thrived from the change, for her mistress liked her and pampered her. But she—the woman—was being maddened by Tabitha's pissing . . .

"May I use your toilet?"

"Of course. First on the left."

Returning, lying down again with a sigh, I say, "Don't tell me you have an original Van Gogh drawing in your toilet?"

She pauses to consider, or remember. "Not a drawing, an etching. One of fifty."

"Jesus! A signed Van Gogh in your downstairs loo! That's real class!"

I hear her light chuckle.

"Poor devil . . . Well, it would have been worse if he'd cut off his cock. I can't bear art any more. It winds around you and throttles you like the Laocoön. It makes you feel things excessively, yet appear feelingless. It costs too much, fucking your life up. There's a character in Henry James who speaks of 'the madness of art'."

"I want you to tell me about Annie."

"Have you got my book? I'll show you it."

> His mother
> the earth was very fat,
> the terrible and lifegiving milk.
> Her voice scolded him, her finger tickled his
> little prick, her body pounded maize.

Her shadow was pounded.
Dying, she

said, Cut out
the coral-between-my-
legs, and take it to the Island of
Twin Breasts. They will make you a helpmeet.
It was a long voyage. From Ani's
womb they made a plump wife,
and from her

clitoris
a slim geisha. From the
nothing in between they made discord.
His wife found Ani Vaverusa's sea-salt
scent on him one night. She moaned, So that's
why you haven't fucked me
more than twice!

Her lament
upset their two growing
daughters.—I am ill, moaned his geisha,
pushing him off.—Ani Senikumba has
your hut and your children. I'm only
your shell-necklace.—He found
himself tight-

bound between
two straining palm-trees. He
had to give Ani Vaverusa
a swollen belly and two wrinkled sagging
udders, and he had to give Ani
Senikumba pearls and
sing her love-

songs. One day
Ani Senikumba
met Ani Vaverusa combing
the beach. They started telling each other some

home-truths.—Old maid, he runs home to me,
and fucks me!—Old cow, this
bundle on

my back is
our son!—Sister!—Sister!
Let's find a sharp flint!—They hurried to
Ani's hut and found him on her bed trying
to get himself erect. Ani! He
shot up ejaculating
milk and fell

back dead. Fruit
of the Distant Sleep and
Flower of the Tangled Root mourned him
on their wedding day. Ani Senikumba
said, It's going to be lonely, why don't
you move in here with your
little boy?

They live so
close the sun hardly steps
between them. Ani pounds the maize and
Ani sings the beautiful worksong. And when
they cry their shy cries, or laugh, the moon
blushes crimson with the
fun of it.

(Ani)

"It was trying to bring the domestic and the sexual together;
but concluding it was impossible. Also, at a more literal level,
it was a dream that Maureen and Denise might become close
friends, so we could all live together. Anna Karenina had the
same dream."

"Yes," she observes, "you are always trying to reconcile
impossibilities."

"True."

"So why does your feline Freud call Denise Ani?"

"I guess I'm changing. When she pounds the maize, so to
speak, I do want to pound her."

"And does she want you to?"

"No. But that's understandable. Because in her own eyes she's never been split. She resents my late discovery."

"Also," she adds, "you should be pounding the maize too, shouldn't you? Only you don't want to."

"No."

I stare out at may blossom.

"It's time."

I collect my son, and when I reach home my daughter, Caitlin, is mowing the lawn. That's good. She pauses for a friendly word with Denise, who is emptying the pool, soaked to the hips. It's good that they're friendly now, and that Caitlin feels able to stay here for a while. A quarrel with her boyfriend, and her mother's cramped house, have yielded some fruit. I recall Frost's *Death of the Hired Hand*:

> Home is the place where, when you have to go there,
> They have to take you in.
>   I should have called it
> Something you somehow haven't to deserve.

We have been brought closer by these weeks of her stay. Seeing her, shapely in sweater and faded jeans, I sense again the link, of reticence and vulnerability, between her and me and my father. Were her voice less like her mother's, she might be his reincarnation—having been conceived during the nights following his death.

NINE

Yanks

Saving my father 3/6 at the Regal and sporting my Field Marshal's badge, I can't understand why he looks sad at having given away the *Geographics*; especially when the next issue is already drifting towards our rocky shore from America.

I sometimes glance at the colourful, exotic pictures, but the articles are boring.

Our furthest journeying is to Restronguet on the Fal, for a week each summer. My stomach caves as Dad puts the shaky old van, borrowed for the week, into first gear for the terrifying descent. If the creek tide is out, we can drive across the beach; if it is in, we shall have to park above the water line and walk through a garden right-of-way. Often it is dark as we descend; I fear a plunge into black waters; if I catch a glimpse of moonlit ripples where the beach should be, cold dread grips my heart. I am haunted by water as we trudge up the sweet-scented path towards the cottage.

Our friend Mona is great fun, but most of the week I'm bored, sitting with them under a Victoria plum tree, staring through foliage at the creek. I don't know why we come, or why I look forward to it; except that Auntie Mona is such good company.

Uncle Harry doesn't appear very often.

> Mona turned all language to a comic
> Amazement at catastrophe barely averted.
> "My *gar*, Harold! What did you *do*?"
> Round eyes puckering to chuckles at a new
> Panic and wonder, "My *life*,
> HARold!" Left every phrase on the rise
> Dazzled in its natural drama.

Nothing happened at the creek
That week each summer. I was puzzled
Why parents didn't need to play, just laugh
In tune with Mona's anguished shrieks
At Harry's bloodies and buggers as he guzzled
The fish he'd caught. The lamp lit,
Harry in bed, Mona did exercises,

Groaned, bumped and thumped, showed how far
Snapped suspenders sank back in the fat.
"I'n it *shameful!*" Whooped her anguish.
"Mona, you're obscene." Kneaded more flesh,
Found more. "AMy!" chuckled and thumped. "My *gar!*
Harold, did you *ever!*" I understood,
Half-asleep in my mother's lap,
Everything aquiver, it was good.

(from *Under Carn Brea*)

Every Sunday we walk to Carnkie. Though I get on well with
my relatives, it's mostly boring. Especially chapel, though
occasionally there is some drama; as when Benny Wearne's
eyes moisten on Easter Sunday: "Look at'n there, upon the
Cross of Glory! The dear of 'm, the dear of 'm. And think of
his poor mother, crawlin' about on her hands and knees, I
expec' she was, beatin' her head on the ground . . . Because
her dear cheel was in *hagony* . . ." I sit by dignified Uncle
Eddie in the congregation. It is a sweet choir, from which I can
clearly pick out my parents' voices. The harmonies are at their
sweetest in the closing Lord's Prayer.

But then there is more singing, around the piano in the
drawing room. And Gerald, my cousin, complains because
Auntie Cecie never fills the cups. "More tea, Cecie!" he
commands irritably, and her tiny legs scuttle out. Her pasties
are full of fat. I hide the pieces under the sofa; but at the
evening's end someone pushes the sofa back.

School is even more boring. It's a relief when lunchtime
comes and I go to Auntie Lilie's house. Once, I start out for
it, up the road, then realise it's only breaktime. I creep back
into school.

A quiet and genteel redhead, Auntie Lilie is married to a fat bald-headed man who regularly, in company, lifts a buttock from his seat and farts loudly. She squirms with embarrassment.

I go through a spell of trapping wasps in jamjars, tearing wings off flies.

I enjoy listening to *Itma*, *Monday Night at Eight*, and Vera Lynn's patriotic songs. But mostly I read. Again and again I devour Robin Hood, the words and the pictures—which show the handsome features of Errol Flynn. His romance with Maid Marion mixes with the overwhelming question of who my sister will choose to marry. Our bungalow has become a home away from home for husky Yanks. I play baseball on Carn Brea, one blue summer Sunday, with the bat and ball one of them has given me.

I've become an American, and also Russian, patriot, following my father. Keenly I study maps in the *News Chronicle*, showing the progress of Zhukov or Patton, and couldn't care less about Montgomery.

The war is all romantic searchlights crisscrossing, stocking seams being straightened, 'We'll Meet Again', chewing gum, heroic feats; someone gives me a Nazi helmet, and I wear it to bed.

In newspapers and newsreels I see the dead and living skeletons of Belsen. Not even a sheltered Cornish boy can see such images without being changed forever.

When *The White Hotel* was published in England early in '81, the *Observer* reviewer was troubled by the Holocaust scenes. She found the book 'precise, troubling, brilliant'. The *Guardian* reviewer thought it a very promising effort; The *Times Literary Supplement* said my Freudian pastiche was masterly, but my own style was pathetic. The *Spectator* believed that a major new novelist had arisen; the *New Statesman*, that I'd wallowed in pornography and violence. *The Times*, in two hundred words, found the novel satisfactory, except for the end, which was 'barmy'.

On the whole I was pleased. It had had a respectable press. I got on with Surkov's feverish womanising.

Then, photographers representing *Time* and *Newsweek* were ringing up, asking if they could drive from London to take pictures. I was puzzled, amused. The first American review came, a full front page piece in the *New York Times*. It was not uncritical; I was slightly disappointed, wondering why Viking, my publishers, were shouting so rapturously about it. *Time*, or perhaps *Newsweek*, said the novel showed fiction's capacity to amaze, and I was a cross between Shakespeare and Sophocles. It's a good thing I don't believe my reviews; though I'm more inclined to believe the bad ones.

John Updike later wrote that the success of *The White Hotel* was a triumph of word-of-mouth. It may be true; I wasn't in the States so I don't know. But I believe much of the credit is due to Viking Press. Their people were so enthusiastic, and worked so tirelessly at expressing their enthusiasm, that they more or less compelled editors to have the book reviewed on its own, at length.

News of its success filtered back slowly to England. My Gollancz editor rang to say Penguin had taken a second look, and thought it might not be quite such a commercial flop. When eventually it appeared as a King Penguin, it topped the paperback bestsellers for six weeks.

Vaguely I knew there was to be an auction for the paperback rights in the States. Around midnight a tipsy call came through . . . "Guess, Don! No, higher . . . higher! Two hundred thousand dollars!" In a daze I walked back into the lounge, where Maureen and our children sat. I told them the news; I laughed and did a jig. The only drink in the house was cooking rum; we drank a celebration. As I drank glass after glass, I started to sob. I couldn't stop. I sobbed from guilt. "People died for that! People died for that!"

At that drunken midnight hour it was little consolation to know that my novel wasn't about the holocaust but about the inextricable mix of good and evil in our white hotel; nor that I had not written it with the thought of making lots of money; all I could think or feel was that if the holocaust had not occurred my publishers would not be celebrating with champagne nor I with cooking rum. Wasn't the English critical reaction—that no one with fewer than three 'A' levels could possibly understand it—healthier for the *book*?

Yet Jews were kind; most Jewish readers seemed to like it, even assume I was Jewish. "Your book is liked by *les femmes, les foux et les juifs*!" smiled a lady-interviewer in Paris. There appears to be some truth in that; though also a lot of women abhorred it. A letter in *Time Out* said I hated my heroine because she was Jewish and highly sexed. Her sexual fantasies enraged what may be called hard-left feminists, though not the softer ones. At readings, usually two or three women would rise to tell me my intimations of female sexuality were false; and others would rise indignantly to say they were true. One woman would tell me privately my poem always made her orgasm; another, that it made her sick.

Since I wasn't attempting to describe all women's sexuality but only one woman's, I took heart from the positive female responses.

Having a book of mine read by (ultimately) millions of people was exciting and fulfilling, yet also disturbing. I had made it simply, as on a potter's wheel. For me it was one object; but my readers shivered it to fragments by their extreme and contradictory reactions. The book was both pure and filthy; I became a guru to some; to others (in the words of a correspondent from Arizona) 'the world's biggest pervert'. I was neither guru nor pervert; but I did feel myself to be torn in two.

Some claimed I had written an exploitative book, tailored to be commercial. Since neither I nor my publishers anticipated commercial success in view of the book's complex and innovative form, this criticism—as my cat Tabitha might wish to say—pissed me off.

Denise at the garden pool, bailing strenuously with a bucket; one large, wet-stockinged foot planted on the patio stones, the other on the pool kerb. Sturdily built, broad-shouldered and broad-hipped, she might be a peasant woman in a Courbet painting. Her ample skirt is sodden, but she doesn't care: devoted to her labour, which she curses. She is no longer the slender girl in a lyrical green suit whom I photographed by Yeats's Tower, at Lissadell, under Ben Bulben, on an early, stolen holiday, though her dark hair is still cut elfinly short. And she stirs me just as much, with a love made stronger by births and deaths and a thousand quarrels. As I approach, she greets me without turning her head from the dark pool water, which she swishes on to the patio and on herself. "Watch out for a newt!" But she herself watches; not a sparrow falls without her knowing it and mourning it. Her thighs so stretched apart, I long to reach up under the wet skirt and touch her where the skin will be the coolest, silkiest, of any I have touched; but Caitlin is near, resting on the mower, and children are as censorious as parents. Besides, it's the last thing Denise would want while she's working, and she's almost always working. She laughs earthily at another splash. A creature of earth and water, she keeps my feet on the ground; though I have not needed her help lately, since my spirit has gone underground. Today, I feel it percolating up to the surface. She blends with the rockery's forget-me-nots and aubretia, its juniper and Flame of the Forest. Like the grass, she has been cut down a thousand times but springs up again, splashed with daisies.

Having encountered the solitude of full-time writing, I preferred the problems of 'success' to the problems of 'failure'. Plato's ghost might sing, "*What then?*", but it seemed better to be known than unknown. I could travel and meet people. The fear of flying which had grounded me for several years was overcome by an invitation to join a day trip excursion of publishers to the Frankfurt Book Fair: to fly there and back in a day made it seem like a safe coach outing, though in fact the risk was doubled. I arrived at Gatwick to find I'd forgotten my passport; I was allowed on the plane and into Frankfurt on the strength of a book with my photo on the jacket.

I couldn't help but be gratified and grateful that my novel had moved many people, had made them lose nights of sleep.

They tended to remember where they were when they first read it—often on a plane in some exotic part of the world, like Nepal. Art and life came very close when a grand-niece of Freud wrote to me from the States. She told me she had identified strongly with Lisa, and had distributed twenty copies to friends. Her aunt, Anna Freud, didn't like the book. The grand old lady had burst into the offices of the Freud Archives, waved in front of the Secretary's nose the fictitious correspondence of my Prologue and demanded, "Where did he get these letters?"

The lines of Goethe which I had chosen at random for Freud to quote, in a letter to the 'Secretary of the Goethe Committee', I discovered had been the precise ones the real Freud had quoted in his address of thanks upon being awarded the Goethe Prize for Literature. Coincidences seem to cluster around *The White Hotel*. While I was chastising myself for being too lazy to observe an operatic rehearsal, the composer Nigel Osborne rang to ask if I would interpret for a Russian conductor at rehearsals of the Welsh National Opera. Osborne had no idea what I was writing. I almost dropped the phone when he mentioned the opera—*Eugene Onegin*. I went; my Russian was hopelessly inadequate; I was sacked. But I had done my research. As a result, I changed nothing in the text. I think novelists can do too much research.

An actress, Ruth Rosen, was performing a reading from my book in Toronto when a Jewish Centre next door caught fire. Recently I visited Milan—eight years too late for research at La Scala. I was shown to a hotel room which I impulsively knew Lisa had stayed in, surrounded by welcoming bouquets. I went down to the lobby and asked my hosts if opera singers stayed there. "Of course. And Verdi died here." A real-life Russian diva, Galina Vishnevskaya, stood for a moment behind my shoulder: so I was told—I didn't see her.

I felt slightly feverish that evening at dinner; and when I went to Lisa's bedroom I was sure something momentous would happen in the night. Maybe Vishnevskaya would come to my room by mistake—or else I would die in my sleep. I slept serenely.

★

I accepted an invitation to teach at the American University in Washington DC in the Spring semester of '82. It was several months away; *Ararat* would surely be finished by then and it would be healthy to take a break from writing, I thought. I could interweave my teaching with weekend trips to promote the American paperback of *The White Hotel*, due out at the same time.

I was asked to take a graduate writing class and a freshman class in the English Novel. They didn't know I didn't know anything about the English Novel. Some months before the semester's mid-winter start, they asked for a syllabus, and I jotted down the titles of a dozen weighty tomes, from *Clarissa* to *Earthly Powers*, that I'd never read but thought I ought to.

I meant to read some of them beforehand, but *Ararat* wouldn't come right; I was paying for the fluency of *The White Hotel*. I had to break off to make trips for foreign promotions. I was in Toronto on the day of the Booker prizegiving in London. At first I had treated it lightly, for I believe writers dignify prizes, not vice versa. But the hype got to me, and now I wanted to win. An attractive journalist was interviewing me in my hotel room, but I was preoccupied. Sean would ring me. The phone rang. My son said, "Rushdie got it." "Fuck," I said.

The journalist said, "If you'd won I was going to take you down to the bar for champagne. But as you've lost, I brought you a consolation prize—" She took from her pocket a little silver maple leaf and gave it me.

The winter that followed was the coldest and bleakest for decades on both sides of the Atlantic. I no longer wanted to go to Washington. I still hadn't read any of the novels I'd have to teach. On the TV news were pictures of an air liner crashing into the frozen Potomac, after taking off from the National Airport. It was described as the most dangerous airport in the United States—and I would have to fly in and out of it a dozen times, because of engagements I'd rashly agreed to with Pocket Books.

Pleading a blizzard, I delayed my flight for two days. Then I descended into a Washington overwhelmed with snow and ice. A jovial Head of English Department met me, and drove me through dark slithery streets to a snowed-up apartment block, a graduate hostel he said was half-a-mile from the University.He used a key to get into the building, then two more to let me into a stark apartment. It was nine o'clock on a Saturday evening, but past midnight by my body-time. I was tired, but hungry even more. I expected him to take me to dinner. Instead, he pointed vaguely in the direction of an area where I would find restaurants, then opened the fridge door. They had stocked it with bacon and eggs, etc., and a bowl of bananas which had turned black because of my belated arrival. For the rest of my stay I displayed the bananas on a table, believing black bananas to be an exotic American variety.

There was also a bottle of bourbon. "Well, I guess you must be tired," said my jovial host. "We'll see you on Monday."

I already felt homesick. Sunday was eerily, snowily silent; but my sanity was preserved by a party given by the generous book editor of *The Washington Post*. On Monday morning I slithered through a blizzard up a hill to the campus. Waiting for me were a score of letters, mostly invitations to speak. I met my English Novel class, and waffled. They gawped at the 'successful author' and I felt a sham, a showman, a shaman. I'd have to start reading *Clarissa*, answering invitations, and beginning a verse translation of *Boris Godunov* promised to the BBC. How could I tackle these tasks when above all I wanted company, and was accepting every half-hearted or warm-hearted invitation to dine? Worst of horrors, I sensed something wrong with *Ararat*, which I had thought finished at last; I would have to ring home and get the typescript sent over.

I struggled down the glacier side with a portable black-and-white TV set someone had said I could borrow.

Clarissa bored me after two pages. Another eleven huge novels after this one . . . In ten days I'd be rushing to a death-trap airport to catch a plane to Ohio. Or Idaho. Or somewhere.

I went out to post a letter, then found I had left my apartment keys inside. I knocked on a neighbour's door; it was opened cautiously on its chain and a bearded, red-eyed Raskol-nikov face glared through the slit. *"Waddya want?"* I stated my problem; he told me the number of the janitor's room and slammed the door. I found the black student janitor wrapped round a tigerish girl. He unhooked himself and a spare key and rose with me in the elevator, breaking the silence only once: "If you need an exterminator, he comes every other Tuesday and Thursday. Let me know."

Exterminator? My mind flashed to Booth, Oswald. Then I realised he meant the cockroaches. But they were my only friends.

I had anticipated something of an Oxford college atmo-sphere: invitations to coffee, a few wild parties. A prison would have been more sociable.

On Wednesday I met my writing class. They were charm-ing and lively. I read to them my verse letter to Andrew, and distributed arty postcards as starting points for a poem. Later I saw the Head of Department and gave him some excuse for needing two long weekends during the semester so I could visit England. He promised to arrange it by doubling some of my sessions. My heart felt lighter; I'd soon have a home leave. And Thursday evening brought a pleasant meal out with two poets. Despite a three-day weekend ahead, with no one to meet, nothing to do except the mountain of work I didn't want to do, I went to bed in a happier mood, thinking, "One week is almost gone. It's not so bad; it's endurable."

When I woke at the usual early hour, still jetlagged, a voice insisted, "You're going home." The command frightened me. I sprang out of bed, lit a cigarette, paced around. The command grew stronger. I leapt into the air with delight, enormous relief. Screw *Clarissa*! I dressed, chuckling, feeling happiness flood through me. I could enjoy to the full my last day in Washington! I murmured love songs to the sweet roaches in the sink as I made tea and toast. Swigging the scarcely touched bourbon, I typed apologetic farewell letters. I told them I was resigning on grounds of future ill-health.

Drunk, I found I had mistyped 'Thank you for your kind-ness' as 'Thank you for your mindless'. I roared with laughter;

I rolled around on my chair and fell to the floor; such tears of merriment streamed from my eyes that I couldn't squeeze shut my lids. It went on helplessly, marvellously; gradually passing into exhausted chuckles.

Pulling myself together, I rang the station to enquire about trains to New York. I wouldn't let Pocket Books down. I'd meet them and re-arrange my publicity trips. They seemed like sanity and fun, even to the key rings promoting my book. Screw academia.

Thinking of keys—what would I do with my three keys? Well, I would leave them all in the locked apartment.

I thought of Andrew in his Oxford hostel. Maybe he had enjoyed his last day like this—stealing away in secrecy.

And indeed my writing students, when my appalling good-bye arrived, remembered my poem about suicide and misinterpreted my drunken regrets. They rushed in a body to the hostel, and feared the worst when they found my door locked.

A rumour later spread that I had a big drink problem. It's about the only problem I don't have.

At the railroad station, I came face to face with a lecturer from the department. She looked puzzled. "You still coming to dinner on Monday?" I said yes, attempting to stand in front of my two suitcases.

I hid myself with an Armenian scholar in the Bronx. I expected, and was willing to accept, opprobrium. The news broke publicly with a long interview in *The Washington Post*; what had been intended as a welcoming piece turned into a farewell: *The Flight of D. M. Thomas*. From all sides—especially from fellow writers—I received warm congratulations.

New York struck me as wonderfully fluid, watery, feminine, after the severe masculinity of Washington: somewhat like Leningrad after Moscow. Pocket Books put me up in a plush Manhattan hotel, and I experienced a hedonistic bliss at floating in room service comfort. Cameras flashed. At the National Book Awards, to which I was invited, a judge pompously said of the still unnamed winner: "We thought to ourselves, This is where we live, this is who we are."

"They're giving it to the Bell Telephone Company!" I said to my Pocket Books hostess, and laughed joyously. It was the first joke I had cracked in a week.

After an appearance on the *Today Show*, I shared the hotel elevator with a befurred middle-aged lady and her daughter. She stared at me. "Didn't I see you on TV this morning?"

I nodded.

"I thought so! Aren't you a writer?"

"That's right."

"Honey, this man was on TV just now! I saw you!" She added inconsequentially, "*And* I was dressing at the time."

TEN

Reds

At ten years old, I have a brush with fame. A schoolmaster instructs me to look after a small, shy, blond-haired new boy. He talks posh; I regard him with due contempt. Playing rugby-touch, I rip his nice pullover. He retires sobbing. He is Richard Sharp. Never, when he threads through a Welsh or Scottish defence, will anyone ever again make him cry.

The war over, rugby has reappeared. A light in his eyes, my father speaks proudly of the mythic pre-war Redruth team; of Jennings, the matchless centre. But when I see Jennings, saying hail and farewell in a charity match, he is a pot-bellied middle-aged man who can scarcely run. But there are other heroes, and every Saturday I sit with my father in the stand, breathless with expectation.

Lois, too, is breathless with expectation. She will not be marrying the craggy American major she was in love with, but the short Australian Flight Sergeant who courted her shyly for nine evenings, earlier in the war. My parents liked but feared the experienced-looking Texan; whereas the Australian, whom they only glimpsed walking up the road with her, is all fresh blue-eyed innocence and writes Christian letters. Ray is sailing from Melbourne for her.

His ship is becalmed in the Indian Ocean because of engine failure; he suffers doubts. On the train from Liverpool, he faints in the crush. He has to change at Truro for Redruth —but in fact 'Bluey' is rushing along the platform, in a familiar camel coat. After drowning him in hospitality, Mum and Dad go to bed early. I too lie in bed, listening to the familiar distant sounds of the American Forces Network. 'Bluey' kicks off her high heels, to look Ray in the eyes, and they dance dreamily. If the tall Texan enters her dream, she doesn't say.

Next day, a Sunday, Ray comes with us to Carnkie and meets our relations. No, they'll give chapel a miss. With winks and banter we leave them to it. To play 'ping pong'.

Auntie Lilie dies, in a hush, of stomach cancer.

Ray goes off to Belfast to learn the linen business. When he returns, it's time for the wedding. On the eve, he floats up the road to Carnkie—so as not to see the bride on her wedding morning—feeling unreal; and half keels over during the ceremony. Uncle Leslie has to steady him with a gruff: "Ray".

In the wedding photos I'm growing a paunch: I dislike my Grammar School, and especially gym, even more than Elementary School, and am over-eating.

They spend their honeymoon in Torquay. Ray reads for a while, turns out the light, and falls instantly asleep: being thoughtful towards his exhausted bride, who lies awake, puzzled and deflated.

But they are very much in love, and she has the excitement of departure to look forward to, after his last spell in Belfast. He returns to the coldest, snowiest winter I have ever known; helps me to make a snowman. Lois's trunk is packed. She thinks it's the end of a Hollywood film, the ride-off into the sunset, with Melbourne not much further than the Isle of Wight. She is still bright as the taxi comes and she kisses her Mum and Dad goodbye. They're not coming to the station.

As the taxi draws away, and we wave from the front room, she bursts into tears, and she goes on crying. Her tears wash her across the world.

The house is sad, silent. A year passes, in which I'm the only boy in England to support Don Bradman's triumphant cricket team. An uncle, my mother's brother, arrives from the States on a visit. He is small, white-haired like her; once a miner, now a Methodist preacher. One evening my parents go out, leaving me with him. He takes paper and pencil, and draws for me a hole. "This is what's called a vagina. And this—is sperm."

"Can it really shoot right across the room?"

"It sure can!"

My parents return home, looking furtive. I'm filled with disgust at what they get up to.

My uncle sails back to America, mission accomplished.

I fly in from America after my cock-up in Washington. The blizzard is over; I meet green fields dappled with snow, and controversy.

An antique dealer, writing to the *TLS*, has accused me of plagiarising *Babi Yar*. Staring at the parallel texts, liberally sprinkled with ellipses, I blanch.

It will have to be answered. Yet I grit my teeth in anger at the waste of energy, at time stolen from *Ararat*. Given the subtleties of a literary work, it takes ten times more energy to answer a charge of plagiarism convincingly than it does to make the accusation. I can't even be bothered to re-read my Babi Yar section. The poet and critic James Fenton, whom I have never met, answers the charge more effectively than I do. I scribble to him an embarrassed note of thanks.

One of the problems is that Penguin, unknown to me, have printed my acknowledgement to Dina Pronicheva's testimony in smaller print and on a separate page from my other notes and acknowledgements. Fenton explains the technical reason for this; but the alteration is regrettable. All the same, I would expect someone intent upon ravaging a writer's reputation to glance at the original hardback.

The controversy fades, and I get on with writing. Except where pure fraud can be proven, charges of plagiarism are foolish and futile. All that matters is whether a work has an original force, taken as a whole; and only time can decide that.

Underlying the intemperate accusations was a serious, interesting issue: to what extent may a writer of fiction use documentary sources? I would say, as much as he feels he needs to, unless art is unrelated to life and history. But my use of Dina's narrative had posed a technical problem, and it was reasonable that others might wish to debate it in a serious way.

There was, I felt, no such justification behind another attack—though the word 'plagiarism' was carefully avoided—which blew up from the United States not long after. This one took me by complete surprise. My translations of Pushkin were being published. These translations had been a labour of love and gratitude, with the certainty of small financial reward.

Translators, said Pushkin, are 'the post-horses of enlightenment'. I was to find that one or two were ill-tempered jades. For myself, I should be happy for any future translator to make use of my versions of Pushkin or Akhmatova. A major poet needs to be re-translated constantly, as language and poetic style change. Previous versions can be stepping stones: nothing matters except to bring the foreign poet alive into one's tongue. There is no place for vanity.

In my case I had made especial use of John Fennell's translations for Penguin, and said so in my acknowledgements. His were prose, mine tried to be poetry. Yet a flood of criticism and backbiting burst when Simon Karlinsky, an authority on the poetry of Tsvetaeva, attacked me in the *New York Times*.

In a West Coast campus newspaper a plump Karlinsky is shown, with an attractive woman, holding open a copy of the *Times* and smiling. In the accompanying interview—which may or may not be accurate—he is described as smiling or grinning on five occasions. He relates how he noted I had acknowledged being 'much influenced' by Fennell; 'padded along to a colleague's room' for his Penguin *Pushkin*; and found—that I had been much influenced!

There was an intriguing remark in the campus paper: Karlinsky, according to the journalist, said Pushkin admired women, whereas I showed a contempt for them. I wondered how he thought he knew that. It could only have been from having read and disliked some of my original work—probably *The White Hotel*. If so, he had not acknowledged the prejudice. Perhaps he thought I had been 'over-generously overpraised'—to quote a telling phrase, about another translator, in his review.

The Pushkin attack left me feeling covered in slime, though not from guilt. Too much unpleasant jealousy had surfaced during the controversy. Since then, there has been one little-noticed accusation which took my breath away. It concerned a short section in *Ararat* where a loathsome old man, Finn, summarises the Armenian massacres by the Turks in 1915, as though he took part in them all. I used and acknowledged the detailed facts and figures provided by Christopher Walker in his *Armenia: the Survival of a Nation*. The historian wrote to a literary journal saying in effect that I had plagiarised his research.

My concern had been to make the Armenian suffering more widely known. I assumed this was his purpose too. Now he was saying he owned the rights—to sentences describing the rape and murder of women and children!

The question was, who owned the rights to a holocaust?

I fly to Finland for the white nights. An open air literary conference. I want to see Finland, not to attend the conference. I begin a novel, *Swallow*, an unorthodox sequel to *Ararat*, which will involve a contest of improvisers by a Finnish lake. For once I'll be able to research my setting. But no, by the time I reach Helsinki I've already written most of the Finnish scenes. I've moved on to Russia. I gaze longingly across the Gulf to where I imagine Leningrad. For so long that granite city, Peter's window into Europe, has complemented granite Cornwall in my creative imagination. Well, soon I'll be there, at last. *Vanity Fair* has commissioned a travel piece and will pay for my trip.

Meanwhile, the conference's setting, by a remote lake, is marvellous; the simultaneous translations into five languages are well organised; but the conference itself is tedious. How absurdly pompous, to stalk up to the mike and declaim, in German or Dutch or Japanese, on the theme of Literature and Science! As if anyone has anything new to say. I certainly haven't, and I don't speak at all during the entire week. I give lots of interviews; and endure a halting, formal dialogue with an uneasy Armenian poet, for *Ararat* has been published. His bloodless KGB ghost listens carefully. Yes, yes, I must visit Armenia someday.

There's no point. I've exhausted it in my imagination. I don't particularly want to see Mount Ararat—though in '84, in Australia, I shall be tempted to visit the Victorian Ararat, a village, simply because it's unknown.

At midnight on the longest day, the Finns play the Rest of the World at soccer. Much beer and wine is drunk; the Finnish girls are as beautiful as the white nights, the shimmering lakes and trees. Yet the most memorable experience of the week is a visit to Sibelius's house, set in a laconic, mysterious landscape that is like a metaphor for his music.

I discovered Sibelius during a National Service Russian Course. After the horror of basic training, I knew I was lucky to find such a comfortable way to spend the two years. I had an 'A' level in French, and a place at Oxford waiting: sufficient background for the Army to train me to interrogate captured Russian soldiers in the next war. I had no interest in Russian; I was homesick and—after meeting a lively and sexy schoolgirl called Maureen at an Old Time dancing class —lovesick; our 'school' at Cambridge might be the highest circle but it was still Hell. Every National Serviceman with any sensitivity thought the same. We wanted to get on with our lives.

I am a poor linguist, but I survived by learning religiously our daily wordlist. One day it might be all the shades of meaning a Russian can express by adding a prefix to *khodit*, to go; another, the various terms for tanks or shells. There was of course a heavy military bias; but our teachers included cultured emigrés, who couldn't avoid giving us a taste of Russian literature. I remember tears streaming from the eyes of a former Bolshoi actress as she read from *Anna Karenina*: Anna stealing home to see her little son, and becoming so upset that she forgets to leave him his presents. We were given the task of choosing a poem and reading it aloud. I chose one by Pushkin. My pronunciation of Russian was decent, and the lyric must have moved me; for someone told me our ageing actress had tears in her eyes again and she said, "That young man—he *must* have Russian parents."

So, amidst the tedium of tanks and shells, I began to get a glimmer of feeling for Russian. But far more thrilling was discovering how to masturbate. I was in a Cambridge cinema watching *The Blue Angel*. The constant sight of Dietrich's black-stockinged scything thighs was too much—I came in my pants. I was intelligent enough to work out that if involuntary rubbing against cloth could do it, your hand should be able to. I spent the rest of the weekend in a toilet, wanking like mad. Nineteen, and already 'courting', I was decidedly a late-developer.

I emerged, exhausted and pale, on Sunday evening, and joined my room-mate, who was listening to a new Sibelius LP. Mixing socially for the first time with well-educated and cultured young men, I learnt a lot from them. Our Officer Cadet Mess was for me a kind of finishing school. Altogether, my National Service was one of the most important—I might say seminal—periods of my life, yet I thought it was Hell.

The year at Cambridge over, we returned to our initial training school at Bodmin: *ultima Thule* for the rest, but for me delightfully close to home and girlfriend. I don't think she and I put my new-found sexual skill to use; we were too shy. I abysmally failed an Officer Selection Board and cut the white tabs from my uniform. I spent my last few weeks in Germany, supposedly taping Soviet tankcrews on manoeuvres saying *"Yob' tvoyu mat! "*—"Fuck your mother!"—but most of the time tuning into the BBC's *Family Favourites*.

For my final test of competence I had to 'interrogate' a thuggish grey-haired emigré. Instead of asking him, *"Kakoi vash cheen"*, "What is your rank?" I demanded, *"Kakoi vash chlyen,"* and was puzzled when he doubled up with laughter. He explained I had asked, "How is your member?"

I was graded 'suitable for low-level interrogation after further training.'

English literature and Oxford claimed me; Russian was forgotten. But *Doctor Zhivago*, in English, stirred me to my soul; and several years later I read in the *TLS* a review of a lyric sequence by Anna Akhmatova. It had been published abroad 'without her knowledge or consent'. A few lines quoted in prose-translation moved me, and it occurred to me that perhaps my small Russian could be used. I sent for *Requiem* and laboriously translated it. I returned to her at intervals in my life, finding my own poetic style purified by these sorties into the studio of a great artist; and increasingly finding that our western literature paled by comparison with Akhmatova's moral grandeur in face of oppression.

> When at night I wait for her to come,
> Life, it seems, hangs by a single strand.
> What are glory, youth, freedom, in comparison
> With the dear welcome guest, a flute in hand?
>
> She enters now. Pushing her veil aside,
> She stares through me with her attentiveness.
> I question her: "And were you Dante's guide,
> Dictating the Inferno?" She answers: "Yes."
>
> *(Muse)*

At long last I am in her city! Twenty years after our first encounter. A steely cold, grey day of late November. The tumid Neva, the Admiralty spire, Hermitage, Winter Palace . . . "With my touch, in my sleep, I could find it." And Pushkin's city! "I love you, Peter's creation! I love your stern, majestic line . . ." The Sphinxes of the University embankment . . . *Egyptian Nights*. Cleopatra . . .

Frozen, I climb on board a tram. Black-coated and head-scarfed babushkas . . . The blizzard pelting . . . But what's this? My body shivers, not with cold but with desire; I'm fifteen, suddenly, swaying in a Melbourne tram, gazing at cool green bosomy girls.

I see almost nothing of the beloved yearned-for city, because I have become obsessed with Australia, those two islanded southern years of my adolescence. I have a lust to re-create as much of it as I can, and am impatient to get home to my typewriter. Screw *Vanity Fair*: I'll write my travel piece in haste and earn myself a kill-fee.

Somehow, when I write down my memories, they don't seem separate from the Finnish and Russian narratives of *Swallow*. The youthful experience, blending boredom and ecstasy, pain and delirium, seems oddly Russian, in fact. Nothing for it but to let *Swallow* contain my memoir, *Sheba's Breasts*, named after my favourite childhood book.

ELEVEN

Voyages

I would read and re-read *King Solomon's Mines*, never failing to be enchanted by the struggle across the burning desert, the ascent to the icy snow-capped peaks of Sheba's Breasts, from which the travellers saw the lush kingdom of Solomon. I trembled as the black warriors, the regiment of the Greys, drew up in their ranks for the battle in which they must die. I shuddered at old Gagool, the witch. I rejoiced when the lunar eclipse robbed her of her prey; I yearned, like honest Good, stout and monocled, to take the comely black girl, Foulata, in my arms.

But above all, Sheba's Breasts cast a spell on me. The twin cones, capped with snow, shimmered beyond the desert. There was a drawing of them in the book my parents bought for me. Those mountains were probably the first breasts I ever saw. They were the first premonition of desire.

When in 1949, two years after my sister's departure for Australia, my parents decided we would join them, a part of my excitement was in following my favourite writers, Haggard and Henty, south, into the unknown.

I think probably my father, besides hungering to see Lois, felt it was almost too late to leave a dead-end job. From having been foreman at a small factory making prefab houses, he had been promoted to works manager. He had a little office, and a secretary; and he wore a suit instead of overalls. Then the owners evidently decided they'd made a mistake in appointing a working-class manager, and brought in someone else. Father went back to his foreman's job on the shop-floor—only now they told the workers he was production manager. They weren't fooled: he wore overalls again.

As my parents and I prepared towards the sailing date—my

fourteenth birthday—I looked forward to the extra, long, Christmas holidays: four weeks at sea, then a week or two in Melbourne before they found me a school. I relished the thought of summer. 'Beverly' was sold; our neighbours took some of our furniture, and also my cat Ginger. It was only when I saw Ginger sitting uneasily on the familiar sofa in an unfamiliar house, and gazing at me wonderingly, that the first tears prickled in my throat. A taxi took us to Carnkie, where we would spend our last night before taking a train to Southampton. I hadn't slept in that house since infancy. A drizzly wind rattled the window. I grieved. In the house where I had been born, I already felt homesick.

Grey dunes of ocean. My body and soul staggering, above an awful emptiness. Seasickness, homesickness; mulligatawny soup and vomit. I gradually got my sea legs, but my soul never lost its seasickness. In the midst of taking a bath, as my mother came in with fresh underwear for me to put on, I burst into tears. I was weeping for our cat. It would be missing us, missing its home next door, and it wouldn't understand. You couldn't explain to a pet; you couldn't send it letters. It would simply, I was sure, be feeling lost and grief-stricken. So I wept in the bath, and Mother tried to cheer me up.

Small boats clustering around us at Malta, Port Said. The glow of fresh fruit; yellows, oranges; the shouts of barter; baskets hauled up on lines, and coins passed down. Sun. Water's dazzle. Natives leaning on hoes, watching us, as we nosed through the Suez Canal. Aden; broiled under the arid red rock. The cabin, beneath the water line—Father and I shared it with six men—airless, breathless. The immense glaze of the Indian Ocean. Dolphins leaping. Icecream on deck at mid-morning. Ping-Pong in the games room. At night, we slept on the boat deck, to breathe. The sea alive with phosphorescence; the sky held more stars than darkness, and they were brilliant and new. I described it all in my first, lost journal.

To my homesickness was added another emotional turbulence, so intense I hardly knew if it was delight or sorrow. In the tiny library below the gamesroom there were no children's books: I was forced to read some adult books. And one day, somewhere in the middle of the Indian Ocean, I stumbled on a shy young woman who allowed a man to pull the cord of her dressing gown, and her breasts tumbled out to his hands. Her breasts, shapely and blushed with pink, spilled out of the dressing gown; he reached for them. She smiled. The shy young woman smiled, and laughed, and was at ease with him. And whatever *nothing* was between her thighs—there where my hair was also growing—lay open to him, revealed. As her breasts spilled out, I felt a surge at my groin: a heavy, thick sweet, aching pressure against my shorts. My shorts were long, but it felt as if my penis would be visible, emerging from a leg of the shorts, if anyone should come into the library. It felt as if my cock was straining to get up to the dazzling sun, the brilliant stars.

This was nothing like my uncle's diagrams.

We spent a day in Ceylon, where my father, homesick also, announced that we would return home at the end of two years. We would have to stay two years, or repay the Australian government for our free passages. The news was like a breath of English air to me, in airless Colombo. My father never drank, but Colombo was so hot he had a glass of lemonade shandy. We took a taxi to Kandy, which was cooler. We looked at a Buddhist temple.

The heat grew still more intense. Several of the passengers didn't mind being dowsed in water to mark the crossing of the equator. By night, the Southern Cross was ablaze. My parents sang 'Wanting You' and 'We'll Gather Lilacs' in the ship's concert. I can see them now, half turned to each other: my father's adam's apple above the brown suit which didn't quite fit, his wavy auburn hair; mother small, plump, smiling, white-haired. Her hair had turned from black to white very early. I think of her soul as silver. I think of my father's as bronze.

They loved singing together, soprano against baritone, and they liked spreading enjoyment. The captain of the *Asturias* signed their programme.

The man pulled at the belt of the shy young woman's dressing gown and her breasts, as round and rosy as the fruit on the boats at Malta and Port Said, spilled out to his hands, for his delight. And that *nothing* between her thighs . . . Another couple, in another novel, bounced on mattress springs. I pointed them out to my father, asking what it meant, and he looked embarrassed and didn't answer me clearly.

Perth. Relatives of my brother-in-law entertained us richly. The Great Australian Bight, stormy, but I had my sea legs now. My body, not my soul. That was still staggering above a chasm. Then Lois and Ray rushing on to the ship almost before we had docked at Melbourne: embraces, tears, giggles. A bewildering taxi ride. A huge, glowing, pineapple spiky meal I couldn't eat for grief.

My father's leathery, tanned, weatherbeaten face broke into a crack-toothed smile one suppertime as he related how a woman had seen him looking in on her, through a window on a high floor of the Royal Melbourne Hospital—yet, pulling off her nightdress, she had calmly washed her breasts in front of him. My father was in his white plasterer's overalls. There were many other immigrants. A White Russian labourer shocked him by telling him how things truly were in the paradisal land of socialist brotherhood.

From the University High School yard, as I ate my lunch-time sandwiches, I could look up at the tall hospital and sometimes catch sight of my father. It was a consolation. Though my new classmates, mostly Jewish I found, were friendly enough, I hated school. I hated my heavy grey double-breasted suit with long trousers, my green cap and tie. They were hot and stuffy, and I was fat. At my Cornish school, I had lost my initial fire as a demon fast bowler as I became stout and lethargic. I told my new classmates, when they were forming a team to play on games afternoon, that I was a batsman. They were impressed by my mythical average of fifty. To my horror, I found myself walking out to open the innings, with an athletic, slim, sandy-haired partner, on a silk-smooth, green park oval. I couldn't feel my feet crossing the turf. I took guard; the bowler strode back twenty paces, and came thundering up. I didn't see the lightning-fast delivery, but it struck my bat in the block hole. The second delivery took my leg stump out of the ground. As I walked back to the pavilion, my suave co-opener walked a few paces with me, advising me how I should have played the delivery. I was not selected for the next match. With three bookish, Aryan classmates I took to picking up tennis, on a dusty court next to their Church Youth Club.

I disliked the earnestness of my classmates, weighed down by bulging briefcases; I refused to give up my satchel. But it was pleasing that they didn't call me Fatty, as my English schoolmates had done, and pleasing that the teachers, some of them women, didn't call me by my surname, in that dehumanising British way. A nice maths teacher asked me my name, on the first day, and I said "Thomas". When she asked if she could call me 'Tom', I blushed and told her my first name was Donald. She shortened this to Don, which I found I liked. It was also nice that I wasn't forced to change, amid sweaty bodies, for gym and team games, but could read a book during gym lessons, and take the tram, past my home-stop, to the Church tennis court. But these were small consolations in the desert of homesickness.

I traced a map of the world, and drew on it the course of our voyage home, in two years' time: Perth, Ceylon, Aden, Port Said, Malta, Gibraltar, then wonderful Southampton. I divided it into twenty-four sections. At the end of the first month, I coloured the first section in with a red pencil. Our ship had hardly left Melbourne, was still moving south, into the Bight; but at least we were on our way, I felt.

All the grownups had jobs. My sister was a secretary, my brother-in-law worked at the linen business. My mother, for the first time in her life, found a part-time job, in a nearby hosiery factory, Holeproof. I would get home first, in the stifling mid-afternoon, and rip off my suit and tie, then sprawl in shorts on my bed. A bundle of comics arrived— *Beano* and *Hotspur*—sent by a neighbouring boy who had bullied me all through primary school. But he sent the bundles of comics faithfully. I lay and read them over and over, yearning.

My mother would come home next, bringing me every day a packet of fat, gluey fish and chips. They weren't anything like the crisp fish and chips we had at home, but they bore the same name. They kept me going till suppertime: usually a roast, since we didn't take to salads, paw paws and passion fruit. I grew even stouter. My sister and mother were also plump, but in a shapely way. My sister, lying flat, kicked high from the lounge floor one evening, and I ogled her rucked-back skirt above her nylons. I didn't realise I was staring—and everyone else, Lois included, was in a jolly mood; but Ray spotted me and shooed me from the room. I slunk out, feeling my face burn with shame, and with a sense of unfairness that my father had been allowed to stay.

There were girls at University High, but I could glimpse only their straw hats above the fence at break times. I was still, despite my uncle's lesson, ignorant. A tall, twinkling-eyed Maltese immigrant—the only crude boy in the class—said a poufter was someone who sniffed the saddles of girls' bicycles. I didn't know what he meant. But my penis would fatten and strain against my grey trousers, in the tram coming home, just from watching the slim Uni High girls in their straw boaters and green-and-white-striped dresses, stretching up to strap, hang. They were so cool, so infinitely far; their bosoms swelled and strained against their cool frocks, tenderly, innocently, driving me wild.

And there was a girl waiting at the school tram-stop one day—but she was waiting for a different tram—who didn't make me erect but made me yearn, as I yearned for England. She had fair hair, cut close to her head, with a fringe; flawless fair skin; and big, candid, intense blue eyes. She didn't notice me, or she disdained the awkward lumpish boy swinging a satchel. I saw her, perhaps, twice more, over the school fence; but her image went home with me every afternoon. The crude Maltese boy told me, with a chuckle, she was called 'Freeza'. I wonder, looking back, if it was because she came on or stood off. Painfully shy, I never thought of getting early to the tram-stop and waiting for her, saying hello to her.

Though the days were awful, endless, a constant gnawing hollow under my heart, the nights were worse. My bedroom was the boxroom, at the end of the second-floor flat, close to the back door and the wooden steps leading down to the jungly back garden. The junk of boxes, crates, trunks, pressing round my bed seemed a natural nesting place for spiders and other jungle creatures: though, to be honest, I never saw one in that room. Separated from the two other bedrooms by the bathroom and a gloomy passage, my room also struck me as a natural place for ghosts to haunt: though again I never actually saw one.

Night after night, terror strangled me as lights were switched out, doors closed, silence fell. My heart thumping, I would wait till I thought Lois and Ray must be asleep; then I would get out of my bed, and creep barefoot along the corridor. I had to pass my sister's room to reach my parents'. The floorboards, the cracked canvas, always creaked just outside Lois and Ray's door, and I would freeze before creeping on. At last I could breathe more easily: I'd push open the door of my parents' bedroom, and they would rarely complain, beyond a few mutters. I thought it was quite natural for my mother to get out and take my place in the boxroom. At home father had lulled me asleep with stories he made up. In Melbourne there were no more stories— simply the huge relief of being safe from ghosts for another night.

I have no memory of changing rooms again in the morning; and I guess Lois and Ray must have known what was happening, and I must have known that they knew. But I persuaded myself that my embarrassing nocturnal journey was a secret from them. One night, however, as the canvas creaked and I froze, the door burst open and my stocky brother-in-law burst out, stark naked. Stunned, we both recoiled. I mumbled something about going to fetch a magazine. He pushed past towards the bathroom, muttering; I found a *Sporting World* in the lounge, and returned to my bedroom. I had to wait a ghost-haunted, spider-threatened eternity before creeping out again, and turning my mother out of bed.

Ray and I rubbed each other up the wrong way. I didn't take to his colonial cockiness; I did my best to irritate him and Lois too. Thus, when they both enthused about Australian Rules Football, I persuaded my father that we should follow Carlton, the Blues, rather than their team, the Redlegs. The Carlton Stadium was close to where we lived, so it was sensible; but my aim was simply to create a bone of contention. On many a weekend, when winter came, Ray and I glared ferociously at each other, felt like strangling each other. I also found that Australian Rules, as they had predicted, would be a reasonable substitute for rugby, till I could watch my beloved Reds again.

With the arrival of our second summer, came the English cricket team. I supported them as passionately as I had cheered Bradman's touring team in 1948. I waved a Union Jack, and again glowered eyeball to eyeball with Ray. Unfortunately the English team was demolished. I couldn't bear to go with my father and Lois to the MCG on the last day of the Melbourne Test, because we had a faint chance of winning. I lay on my bed all day, listening to the commentary on the wireless.

By now, 'my bed' was my parents' abandoned double bed, for they had decided to change rooms with me. There was no space in the boxroom for clothes, so they had left those behind. When I opened the wardrobe door, to move the red line an inch nearer Ceylon, I was faced with my mother's floral dresses, my father's brown Sunday suit. And one drawer of the old chest-of-drawers, under the old wireless, was crammed with mother's corsets and brassières and long pink elastic-kneed bloomers. The change, far from being pleasant, brought deeper horrors, deadlier nightmares. For one garish morning I woke to see a palm-size, black tarantula on the walls between the open window and my bed. All my hairs stood on end; I leapt out, and backed away to the door, never letting my gaze stray from the loathsome creature. I hammered on Ray's door. Chuckling, he brought a spray gun; while I cowered near the door, he pumped a sick-sweet gas up at the gigantic spider. Slowly it stirred, sidled, lurched down the wall in a diagonal line.

From that morning my imagination was never free of tarantulas. They swarmed into my bedroom every night, as the spiders in a Dennis Wheatley novel—one of my sister's books—swarmed over Toby Jugg, paralysed, the victim of a coven. I expected, whenever the moon was at full, framing the tree of jagged leaves outside my window, the mother spider of all spiders to crawl in, as it did for Toby. In a quiet suburban street, with a neat park or 'paddock' across the road, I felt surrounded by a jungle. The sweat that poured off me, that indecent summer of 1950, both from heat and fear, could have washed us back to England.

School, and the bedroom where I read, feared and fantasised —this became my life. Ray and Lois hinted that we might settle down better if we had a flat of our own, but Father and I had no intention of settling. Perhaps my chameleon mother, happy wherever her family was, could have settled; but my father killed off all discussion by riding into the city one Saturday morning and booking our passages a year in advance. Then he and I saw a film, as we always did on Saturday morning, followed by a cricket match, or football match in winter, at the Carlton Oval. I liked Saturdays, and especially that one, when our return was made certain.

Yet every inch, every month, on my world map stretched out like a year. I was becalmed. Every day lasted a week—and every night too. Only the evenings were tolerable, when I shut myself up after supper in my room, sprawled out on my bed. The tree was harmless while the light lasted, but dragged my eyes towards it as dusk passed into darkness. I knew the tarantulas and the ghosts were preparing. Dread swept over me when the wireless in the lounge was switched off, or when Lois stopped playing 'The Rustle of Spring' on the piano and I heard the piano lid being closed. Mother would come in to take fresh clothes, and to give me a goodnight hug. Lights went off; bedroom doors closed; tarantulas rustled in the silence. I kept the light on, though the glare added to the intolerable heat and stuffiness. I lay naked, drenched in sweat, and opened my eyes every minute or so to see if a tarantula had come in. A mosquito whined; I searched for it, clapped my hands and it died. I drowsed fitfully; every time I woke I turned my head to the white wall, by the window. My greatest nightmare, though, was to find a tarantula poised right above my head. That never happened. Indeed, very rarely did a spider come in at all.

If I survived until sunrise, I could relax a little, turn out the light, and drift asleep in the fresher early-morning atmosphere. Somehow I expected the tarantulas, as well as the ghosts, to come in the darkness, not at dawn. Yet in reality, dawn was when they came, if they came at all. I never saw one enter, never saw black legs appear round the window frame. They were either there, or not there, when I woke finally to the radiant, already hot, light.

The second or third time when my nightmare became real, I sat on the lounge sofa, recovering, yet knowing I would see that spider all day and into the next night. The sun poured through the window and burned through my white shirt into my back. The others had left for work. I would soon have to walk down to the tram-stop at the end of the avenue. I felt, or saw, a shadowy creature emerge between my black shoes . . . looked down, and jumped out of my skin. It was not the ghost of the first tarantula, but another, immense, evil, walking out into the light of the fawn-coloured carpet. It crossed the room almost to the gas fire, then stopped. I wanted to rush out of the house, but dared not leave it in possession, to vanish. Shuddering, panting, I took the biggest book I could find, approached the spider, and held the book a couple of feet over it. The book dropped with a thud—a flash of movement but not quick enough, thank God. I left the book there for someone else to take care of.

I shuddered, all the way to school. Surrounded by green blazers—happily we had been permitted to discard our grey suits—I still saw the two tarantulas.

★

"Most teenagers," she says, "rebel by going out a lot, mixing with others, wearing their own special clothes, separating themselves as far as possible from their parents. You didn't; you went in on yourself."

"But this was 1950," I protest. "Before the youth culture."

"I know that. All the same, your behaviour was unusual. You were a part of the household and yet apart."

"That's true. I still have the home-seeking impulse, very strongly, yet I need my study to be separate."

"As it is: an extension."

"Yes. I suppose I set up a pattern. In that bedroom I felt myself to be between two worlds: the life of the family, which was calm and cosy; and the life of the tree, which was sinister, threatening, spider-filled."

I glimpse, through my analyst's window, black jagged leaves against the full moon, preparing to send out the tarantulas.

"But you made a false distinction. The family wasn't at all calm and cosy; you glimpsed the turbulent emotions when your sister did her floor exercises, showing herself off to everyone. You, your father, her husband . . . And outside it wasn't *really* sinister, was it? The spiders hardly ever came in, and they were harmless."

"You're right!"

"Spiders are thought to symbolise the female genitals; you know that, of course."

I see the whirl and thresh of plump, white, black-suspendered thighs, framing that thinly, damply veiled unknown.

"It's time."

Dreamtime

Sexual craving—or rather, craving for woman, girl, her touch, feel, scent—burned me up, like the forests of ghost trees in that summer of bush fires. Unlike the colt, Man Shy, I read of in class at about that time, I was fat, yet also stumbled through a desert, parched. I found only the salt water of images: the tight belts and straining sweaters of the page-boyed young women on celluloid or in film magazines; the slenderer bosoms of the summer-dressed, straw-hatted girls on the tram, who never appeared to sweat, and who never looked in my direction; even the matronly models, almost as old as my mother, advertising Berlei or Gossard girdles in the conservative *Age*; even Corky, a good-looking young house-wife, who attached a milometer to her suspender, for the *Australasian*, to find out how far a housewife walked in a day—it was, I think, seven miles. And, once, a chance reve-lation of my sister, her red hair trapped in her slip. I rushed from her room, which I had expected to be empty, and threw myself on my bed, embarrassed, shocked, my face aflame. She came in to see me, when she was clothed: blushing a little too, but also smiling, generous in wanting to make light of it.

I spent quite a lot of time in her room, during the long holiday, or after school before Mother came with the fish and chips. Then I started to 'minch', or play hookey, from school. I was still terribly unhappy there. I had fiddled my end-of-year report to make it look as if I was high up in the class, but I was far behind the serious and intelligent Jews, who had ambitions to be barristers and brain surgeons. I refused to sing, at assembly, an oath to serve the school *strenue ac fideliter*: with zeal and loyalty. So I stayed away from school; or else—on mornings when my mother left later than I—hovered in a lane behind the house, and then crept back in through the rank, tarantula-filled garden. I carried out secret puberty rites in my sister's room which, with the curtains drawn, was cooler than mine, and impregnated with woman scents. It was my dreamtime. Man Shy, who brought tears to my eyes, was my totem. But these rites, too, were salt water, and I went on burning. It never occurred to me to masturbate; I didn't know how. My only orgasms came at night, in entanglements with some unknown woman or girl. They woke me, drenched in sperm and sweat, and I turned my eyes to the white wall by the window.

One morning my sister, unknown to me, had stayed in bed, nursing a cold. She heard the back window scrape open, then steps coming heavily up the passage; she saw the knob turn and the door slowly open towards her; she lay paralysed with terror. I, too, was horrified when I saw her in the bed. The encounter brought to an end my minching from school, my forged absence notes. She asked me if I had been told about sex, and I briefly considered asking her if she would teach me, show me what it was all about. I was not conscious of being hung up on my sister; she just happened to be there. I craved the blue-eyed girl whom I never saw; I wanted Doris Day and June Allyson; the cool girls strap hanging on the tram, UHS emblazoned on their blazers; the husky-voiced woman who, evening by evening on the Top Ten, sang 'Temptation'.

After the Popular Top Ten there was sometimes a Classical Top Ten, always with the Warsaw Concerto and 'Claire de Lune'. The programme was introduced by the solo opening of Rachmaninoff's Second Piano Concerto. Those slow, sombre, wide-spaced chords, gradually growing louder, made the hairs stand on my nape, like the night tree.

I listened to these programmes alone in my bedroom. I had withdrawn into myself entirely, enjoying solitude until night fell. I did my homework—a little more keenly as time went on; glanced through comics—though I no longer read them avidly; carried on with my scrapbooks of filmstars and sporting heroes: longing for autumn and sight of the Blues again. But the temperature went on rising still higher; for weeks it was over the hundred. Fierce, hot winds blew the dust of the tennis court into my eyes, once every week.

The heatwave ended with wonderful suddenness. A forecast one Sunday morning of a breeze from the Antarctic, reaching the city at four—and within minutes of that hour we felt a coolness touch our bare legs and red-hot faces, saw the curtains blow. Energy flowed back into us; we chuckled, went to the balcony to fill our lungs with cooling air. In no time, the mercury had dropped ten or fifteen degrees.

I was starting to do better in school. An acerbic art teacher played us a record of Tchaikovsky's *Francesca da Rimini* tone poem and, without fully understanding what it represented, I painted a flamboyant picture which impressed him.

A resonant, thrilling voice over, in *The Blue Lagoon*, expressed Jean Simmons' newly discovered emotions as she feared that her fellow castaway was drowned . . .

> I wonder, by my troth, what thou and I
> Did, till we loved: were we not weaned till then,
> But sucked on country-pleasures, childishly?
> Or snorted we in the seven sleepers' den?

So this, I thought, is poetry . . . So this is love . . . And I was stirred, equally without understanding, when a student teacher from the University struggled through *Pied Beauty* and *The Windhover* with us. I must have said something sensible, too, because I heard she was asking who the American boy was. Well, a Cornish accent is not so far from an American.

Another bundle of comics came, but I didn't open it.

Time moved more quickly, once the Blues took the field again, amid roars of forty thousand fans. Sitting by Father, I was in an ecstasy of excitement. The way they flew high to bring down the mark! Then the huge punt, taking the ball between the centre-posts! Every Saturday, almost, through the too-short season, Carlton won. They came out on top, and the Grand Final seemed a formality. It was the most thrilling day of my young life, among a hundred thousand at the MCG; and also the bitterest disappointment. No one could remember a final won and lost by seventy-two points. My brother-in-law, to his credit, didn't rub it in.

Our ship had squeezed through the Suez Canal; the journey ahead was so short I no longer bothered to extend the red line on the first of every month.

Spring passed into summer again. The nights were warm, but not yet unbearable. Though I still kept the light on, I found it easier to sleep. If I was woken at dawn by a wet dream, I was happy—once I had checked that there was no tarantula—to lie peacefully watching the light brighten around the tree: grey at first, then pink, then a kind of green, till the sun burst into my room, filling it with another day's warmth. I could see that the picture I had drawn, after *Francesca da Rimini*, had been a representation of the tree.

There were no tarantulas in that last, shortened summer.

I surprised everyone by coming first in my class, the only foreskinned boy in the first ten. The Jews took it good-naturedly. And after the long vacation came another pleasant surprise: the straw-hatted girls from over the fence were now sitting in my classroom. A tremulous, respectful silence fell on us boys when one of the girls bravely said, "Come to my woman's breasts . . ."

I fell hopelessly in love with a graceful, slim, light-footed girl called Sara. She appeared in only two or three of my classes, each day; was often absent through sickness; and spoke to me only two or three times during those few weeks—to ask if she could borrow my biology notebook to copy notes she had missed, and to thank me on returning it. But her shapely, animated face, her gay smile, her step which did not seem to touch the ground, filled my days and nights. If she happened to sit in front of me, the sight of her short black hair converging to a point on her slim nape made me feel weak. I could hardly guide my pen over the paper. During the arid classes we did not share, there were moments of pure grace when she appeared unexpectedly, walking along the windowed corridor; and one weekend—the weekends were unbearably long—her picture, to my amazement and joy, was on the front page of the *Age*, with a caption saying that she loved snow and was skiing in the mountains. I pretended she was my girl-friend, and Ray teased me amiably.

I was blind to everyone else's emotions. The family began to talk, in a kind of tearful, cheerful way of how my/my parents' room might become a nursery after we had gone. I burst into tears over the passion fruit one evening, and said I've changed my mind about going home. I wanted to stay; they could leave me there. They were alarmed, disconcerted; Mother mumbling that perhaps I could live with Ray's parents. But I didn't fancy that; and of course it was impossible, I knew I would have to go. On my last day at school I summoned up enough courage to speak to Sara, saying I was going back to England. We shook hands politely, while my heart was breaking. I thought to ask if she would mind my writing to her, but was too shy.

Before we left, Ray was going to take Bluey for a short holiday up-country. It would provide a distraction for her. To break the gloomy atmosphere, as they waited for the taxi, I played a lugubrious piece on the piano. But an ache of grief gathered in my throat when we ourselves, the next day, passed in a taxi along by the Blues' stadium, desolate in the bright, midsummer sunshine; and passed the tram-stop near my school. Sara was in there . . .

Dolphins, and table tennis. A girl who sat at the next table in the dining-room seemed to want my company, but she didn't appeal to me. I was dazzled by a blue-eyed, corn-haired New Zealand girl. She was eighteen, travelling with her mother. She was much too old for me, of course, and was in fact going to meet her fianceé in London. I ignored her courteous indifference, and haunted her and her mother. I would squat with my copy of Shakespeare's Tragedies, which I couldn't understand, close to her deckchair. From heat, tennis, Sara, the abandonment of fish and chips, and now the shipboard passion and strenuous table tennis, I grew slimmer.

I recall almost nothing of our home-coming; the train journey from London; our welcome at Carnkie; settling into the family house. It was cold, drizzly, and I mourned for Sara.

A couple of weeks after our arrival we walked the familiar road to 'Beverly'—forever lost—to call on our ex-neighbours. Before the bungalows came in sight, my father whistled for Ginger, as he had always done. It was just a sad, nostalgic joke. But there was Ginger, bounding down the road towards us—as if not a day had passed. We stroked her—and never saw her again.

As painfully as I had settled to Melbourne, I adjusted to the life of a village and of the patriarchal house.

T H I R T E E N

Trees

The plane drones on. The journey is endless. Phantoms weave
on a screen in front of me in the darkened cabin.

I sip a vodka and martini. This, and the sense of hurrying
forward in time, into night, bring back Russia, two years ago.
The evening with Yevtushenko and his pleasant, quiet English
wife; the walk in gumboots to Pasternak's grave. Grey,
turbulent Neva; gazing down at its reflected lights, thinking of
Akhmatova and her sorrows; striding through war graves,
quoting *Requiem* aloud, tears stinging my eyes. Her spirit, and
Pushkin's, at Tsarskoye Selo. Craving for coffee as the bitter
wind stung me; and for a cigarette on the guided tours.

The phantoms on the small screen become others. A grey-
haired woman weeping over a telegram is my grandmother.

The group standing around a grave becomes a crowd in
cloth-caps and black bonnets waiting at Redruth station for the
train, bringing him home . . . I guess my grandfather must
have played the organ at his funeral . . . The chapel would
have been packed. Such a young man, so lively and popular. If
God intended us to fly, He would have given us wings . . .

Earphones plugged in uncomfortably, I listen to a Branden-
burg Concerto. Bach doesn't turn me on, but I keep trying.

I'm exhausted, and sleep would pass the time; but the mild
sleeping pill isn't working.

We're over the Middle East. *Cleopatra e i suoi amanti* . . .
Uncle Eddie always talking about Mespot. I can't imagine him
in puttees, wielding a rifle, such a gentle man, like them all.
The pipe, the politely doffed trilby . . .

Ah! This is better than Bach: the dry voice of Sigmund
Freud . . .

★

At his third or fourth visit, the Spiderman—as he became known to me because of his terror of spiders—offered me some details of his paternal ancestry. He had gathered the information from a number of sources: including an aged but sharp-minded distant relative; family rumour; a Family Bible; a South Australian lady, writing to him out of the blue; and a dubious firm of genealogists—so dubious that they at first told him his grandfather had been a butcher from St Austell, whereas he knew him to have been a mine-carpenter living at Carnkie, near Redruth.

His great-great-grandfather, Richard, born around 1800, was a miner and not inconsiderable landowner, owning a rich slice of farmland at Truro, an inn and farm at Carnkie, as well as other properties. The patient saw him as perhaps a Poldark figure, venturing in tin and making good. He had a brother, William, married to a half-French lady, who mined in South America for a time, then in 1828 sailed on the *Royal Admiral* for Adelaide. There he set up as an innkeeper. One of his descendants was said to be Mary Durack, a West Australian historical novelist.

Richard's eldest son, of the same name, married a 'titled lady' and then his housekeeper. He built 'Treliske', a manor house at which he entertained the Prince of Wales. A second son, William, Thomas's great-grandfather, married a woman who was half-Italian: thus possibly explaining the strongly Italian looks of some members of the family. According to family gossip, which rarely lies, the ancestral Italian was an artist who had come to paint a mural at Tehidy Manor; his wife, or mistress, mother of twin girls (one of them Mary Jane, Thomas's great-grandmother), 'never smiled again' after he deserted her for his warm native land.

Mary Jane Thomas, blending the Latin and the Celt, was rumoured to have been very beautiful. William was a carpenter who also ran the inn at Carnkie. It is said he drank away their money. They tried their luck in America, but he didn't like the New York skyline so, without landing, sailed home in the same ship. This trait was to be passed down to his great-grandson, my patient.

The self-ruined man lived in and ran a small village-shop in Carnkie. It would have gone hard with his eldest son (also William) had not fate taken a kindly turn; one of his aunts married a mine captain, Josiah Martin, and they died childless. Their substantial Victorian house passed to the indigent William. With his wedding to Eliza Bennet of Troon in 1881 the huge Family Bible appears; gossip and parish registers give way to a carefully recorded family tree as well as to living memory.

Burdened with twelve children, of whom only two failed to survive, they were poor but blessed with a house which dwarfed its neighbouring terrace of tiny miners' cottages. Daily the Victorian brood must have gazed in gratitude at the gloomy portrait of Josiah Martin, founder of 'St Martin's Villa'. The saintly character of Eliza Thomas quite overcame any local envy; she was worshipped by her children. One of the signs of her influence was that none of them drank, though drink had apparently 'run' in their family hitherto.

William—Billy—was a more complex character. He was obviously Italian in looks (of the short fat kind) and in mannerisms and characteristics. He was bubbling over with music. Indeed, he would escape to the dining room to play the American Organ for hours. He carved the pews for a new Methodist chapel, and became organist: performing with such vigour that he rocked to and fro in ecstasy. Most of the young members of the congregation could scarcely suppress their giggles. In the vestry afterwards, it was hinted, he fondled his daughter Cecie. He led Eliza a hard life: she is unsmiling in photographs; immensely sad. He would sail off to find work in South Africa, find a mistress also, and his family wouldn't know when to expect him back. He could draw sensitively; and loved his carpentry so much he said he 'ran to his bench every morning'. Yet his sons would joke: "He's heard a voice say, 'Work no more'."

The children, and especially the sons, were good-looking, intelligent, talented and industrious. The collapse of the mines on which the village depended—which indeed had created it—forced many of them to go abroad for work, thus broadening their minds. Yet, as regards family life, most of them were denied complete fulfilment.

Ethel, a large woman of florid Italian good looks, married a humble miner and raised two beautiful daughters. All three, however, and Ethel's little grand-daughter, died of tuberculosis. Whether or not the tragic woman felt she had paid a grievous penalty for an adulterous relationship with a mine captain, she became understandably depressed in later life, until a happy second marriage.

Of the four children who travelled to California—Lilie (accompanying a husband), Harold, Leslie and Percy—the last-named never came home. Childless, Percy and his stout, singularly unattractive Californian wife adopted a baby daughter.

Lilie was married to a vulgar man who constantly embarrassed her. She died in middle age, without children. Leslie, another striking 'Italian', married happily but was denied offspring. William, who went mining in South America in his youth, returned home to marry a neurotic *belle* (which was actually her name), and settled down to become a printer's agent in London. His wife would fall ill whenever he planned a Cornish holiday; he retired with her to Cornwall when effectively it was too late, for most of his family had died.

Eddie, after serving with the Army in Mesopotamia, worked as a men's outfitter; his young wife died, leaving a son, Gerald. They were looked after by Cecie, who never married. Nellie lost her fiancé in the war, served in a sweet shop, and developed crippling arthritis. Donald, a merry and mischievous youth, auburn-haired like Harold and Lilie, joined the peacetime Air Corps, and crashed to his death on Salisbury Plain.

Of them all, only the patient's father, Harold, born at the turn of the century, had what might be termed a normal family life, with wife and natural children. He had artistic talent, but was forced to train as a fitter. At twenty he sailed for Los Angeles, returning later to claim his childhood sweetheart, Amy (*née* Moyle). They were married on Easter Saturday, attended a rugby match in the afternoon, and left for America in the evening. She was seasick for almost the whole voyage.

Despite that inauspicious beginning, their marriage was for the next six years sunlit—literally and metaphorically. It was the founding era of Hollywood; Harold helped to build Rudolph Valentino's house; then built his own attractive Spanish-style bungalow in Beverly Hills. Doubtless, had they stayed in California, their property would by now have been worth a fortune. But depression struck America, and struck his mother—with the tragic death of her last-born son, Donald. The young couple, with their four-year-old daughter, returned home.

The influence of democratic America never faded. When an English boss called curtly, "Thomas!" Harold replied, "I've got a handle to my name." Amy became absorbed into her husband's family at 'St Martin's'. She kept her own family at a certain distance. Apart from one aunt, the Spiderman rarely saw his mother's people; he knew little more than that her mother had died while she was young, and she had been raised by an older sister, who herself died prematurely. Two of her three brothers had emigrated to the States. The Spiderman had grown up overwhelmingly within the atmosphere of the paternal family; continually he contrasted the simple virtues of their lives and characters with the complexities of his own.

". . . Hi! This is Sara."

"*Sara!* Good heavens! Hello!"

"Welcome to Aussie!"

Her voice sounds much more stridently Australian than it did thirty-three years ago. Or rather, I don't recall her voice, only her graceful face and form, her dancing black eyes, and steps that glided on asphodel.

Intrigued by a poem I'd written about her, a Melbourne editor had looked up Sara's uncommon maiden name in the directory, and spoke to her mother. Put in touch with Sara, I had written and she'd replied, with a photo. She was still recognisable, still attractive. But she didn't remember me at all.

Now she was on the line to my Adelaide Hotel: "I saw in the *Age* you were at the Festival. You must come and have dinner with us when you're in Melbourne. My daughter would be thrilled; she's read your book— *The White Hotel*."

"I'd like that. I'd love to see you."

"Yes, it would be beaut."

"I'll ring you when I know what my publishers have got lined up for me in Melbourne. I'll only be there a couple of days."

Though I've dreamed of Sara for thirty-three years, already I'm preparing the ground for a withdrawal. It's the word 'beaut' which puts me off, makes me realise the memory of her early image is too precious to risk losing. It would be terrible if I fell for her daughter.

In Adelaide, March '84 was hot and cloudless: late summer. The long flight south had seemed endless, yet scarcely as many hours as we had spent days on the post-war voyage. In the boarding lounge at Heathrow, I overheard an unhappy woman denouncing England's weather. A childhood emigrant like me, she had returned to England to see her parents, but her father had died during her stay. She couldn't stand the cold and rain, so she was returning home early.

Lois had come to Britain in '75, just too late to see her mother. She had flown back via Los Angeles, and liked it so much she decided to stay in the place of her birth. How mysterious were the patterns, the lines drawn by fate or providence or chance. And her son Lloyd, my nephew, had decided to live and work in Glasgow, of all places!

I myself felt that I would be met in Melbourne by a kind of twin more bronzed and leathery than I, and with a colonial twang. He would introduce me to his charming, cultured wife, perhaps a Greek, and to charming children. They would take me to a nice bungalow in Moorabbin or Ivanhoe. He is perhaps a University lecturer, and he writes. His wife has taught him some Greek and he has translated Cavafy. Has he written a novel called *The Blue Motel*? Over a midnight drink, when our polite conversation is already dragging, he hints jokily, uneasily, of complications in his life. For he grew up in the same atmosphere of intimate distance, cautious intimacy. Afraid of ghosts and spiders—he still fears and loathes tarantulas—he slept with his father. He watched our sister kick high from the lounge-floor—sexually, we find as the conversation warms up, we are quite alike.

He doesn't know Russian, and has never read Pushkin or Akhmatova in translation.

A nostalgic expression crosses his face as I talk of my vague plans to move to Cornwall. Though his vocabulary is full of Australianisms, 'sheila' and 'drongo' and 'footy', he still feels vaguely Cornish.

Rushing towards that twin, in the Club Class of a British Airways airliner, scything across continents and oceans, suffering disturbances of light, I am overcome by the sense that time and the world are an illusion. Far below, where the blue Pacific shimmers, the *Asturias* goes on churning towards Australia. A fat fourteen-year-old, running in sweat, waits impatiently for the mid-morning serving of icecream on deck. Then—if there is a then—the world was inside me, I could grow it as I pleased; now—if there is a now—it is outside me and I am helpless to change it. We have lived through the Berlin Wall and Korea, Vietnam and Cambodia, space-probes and organ-transplants, sexual revolutions and retrenchment. The Kennedy brothers have been murdered, and new viruses have been born. What *improvisatore*, I wondered, had spun that narrative, and why? The curving glittering ocean turned to me the face of a sphinx, and a new novel stirred in me.

And my own infinitesimal and infinite life—the sphinx had shaped that too . . .

The comfortable hotel-room in which I took Sara's call looked down on a dilapidated Egyptian restaurant marked with the figure of a sphinx. The theme of my coming novel became less murky: it would be *murk* itself, the sphinxes of love and history, smiling at our pathetic attempts to clarify them with left-or right-wing values and ideologies. Writing about it might mean squirming through a labyrinth of tunnels or mine adits, like Quatermain in the land of Solomon and Sheba. I might never get out.

I appeared, when necessary, at the Arts Festival, mostly strolling round the edges of the marquee, chain smoking and preoccupied. My agent called from London to tell me about an historian's complaint that I had stolen his Armenian corpses. A woman approached me to say she liked my work, and told me a harrowing story. Her teenage daughter had disappeared from home, and two years later had been found, with six other corpses, in a paddock near the South Australian Truro. Mrs Mykyta gave me a copy of the book in which she had described her nightmare: *It's a Long Way to Truro*.

In spite of that title, Cornwall seemed close, closer than to Hereford. Cornish miners had come in droves in the last century, and played a large part in founding the State. A High School class to which I read and talked had three children with solidly Cornish names, who knew all about their ancestry. This High School visit was my happiest experience in Adelaide, though the one I had most feared. Their English teacher, an animated woman of Greek origin, had well prepared the fifteen-year-olds. They joked with her, called her by her first name, Anna; they listened to mildly erotic passages with lively, humorous appreciation; maturely, without prurience. It took me back to my class at University High—not unlike this one, except we were all boys till the Fifth Form. Afterwards, while I was chatting in the staff room, one of the girls brought in a tray of crockery; interrupting our chat with a tactful "Excuse me," she said, "Mr Thomas, I just wanted to tell you we all enjoyed it; it was wonderful." Then she flitted away.

In England I have read to rebellious louts and stiff-necked Public Schoolboys, all equally suspicious of poetry and feelings. For any of them to have thanked me with such spontaneous courtesy would have been unimaginable. Perhaps I was lucky in my school, chosen for me at random; but it confirmed an impression of relaxed, classless warmth in Australia. I didn't miss the England of Scargill and Badminton.

But Melbourne, when I reached it, had turned into an unrecognisable American city. Flashing XXX porno-signs in staid Collins Street. I recognised the family features, auburn hair and freckles, in my niece. She had shot straight from being a dream in Lois' and Ray's mind, when we left, to being a shy, independent bachelor girl of thirty. She drove me out of the city along Princes Park. Hazy memories, of the park, my school tram-stop, the Carlton stadium, came into focus poignantly. I had forgotten the lines of trees, the cycle tracks. She turned left into our avenue, slowing in uncertainty. Angela wasn't sure if the house where she had been born was still there; and evidently didn't care. She had been spared my family sentimentality. I looked for a slender tree growing at the side, brushing against a second-floor window.

Several houses have been destroyed to make way for a motel; maybe ours is among them. But no, there's the tree! We stop and get out. I stare with turbulent emotions at the drab red-brick house. The tree is different; it's lost its jagged jungle leaves; those dusty, listless leaves cling to nothing more exotic than a copper beech.

I wonder if there are any shreds of me still in the second-floor flat. Perhaps at the back of some cupboard there's a torn page of *Photoplay* or of my story about feeling-up Princess Margaret; or Sara's picture cut from the *Age*.

In *Sphinx*, I sent my exiled Russian, Barash, to live in that flat; I visit him there. Actually there was a brass plate, indicating a lawyer of probably Yugoslavian origin. We drove away. I was silent, listening to my parents singing. Angela dropped me off at the school tram-stop, promising to pick me up in half-an-hour. A green tram clatters along, reminding me of Leningrad. It's a cloudy, heavy, listless day; I have forgotten there were such nondescript days. Sprinklers whirr, spreading a sharp scent of freshened grass which cuts through all memories and forgetfulness like the madeleine in Proust whom I must someday read.

I had forgotten, but remembered swiftly, the paint-peeled ornamental balconies of the Victorian houses lining the short, quiet road to the school. The façade of the school itself seemed entirely strange; it came back slowly. The late afternoon was silent. School was over. I walked through into the playground where I had eaten my sandwiches and gazed up at the Royal Melbourne Hospital to find my father. There was no hospital. I assumed a new building was in the way.

Returning to the tram-stop, I expected the girl with short blonde hair and candid blue eyes to be waiting there, indifferent to me. Tears pricked my eyes.

Nirvana

Tears prick my eyes, remembering Sara. I wonder if she ever thinks of me.

I loathe my old school, its male smell, rowdy boys, ATC parades, moustached ex-RAF schoolmasters; loathe having to wear the tight cap. In class, I think always of Sara's slender nape in front of me. School friends I jealously cherished just two years ago—now I barely acknowledge them. Not out of rudeness; our worlds have become different.

From summer, blue skies, a teeming city—winter, cold and drizzle, a tiny barren village. And the whole desperate loss and homesickness is imaged in the face and form of Sara.

Our solid granite house, 'St Martin's', stands below the Methodist chapel; on the other side is a straggly terrace of miners' cottages. We face open fields, mine ruins and bleak Basset Carn. Behind us are more fields, more ruins, Carn Brea with its Monument and Castle. At the top of the village is a newly built Men's Institute; at the bottom, a pub. It's referred to almost in whispers in our house, as if it were a bordello, though my great-grandfather had owned it. There is a tiny Primitive Methodist chapel for enthusiasts, and a village post office, run by our cleft-palated chapel organist.

'St Martin's', although it is not huge, although it has no bathroom except in the extension my father is building, and although we are poor, manages somehow to maintain an Edwardian dignity and serenity. The sloping lawn is secluded within privet and shrubs; the dining room and drawing room are hushed, venetian-blinded.

Auntie Nellie and Uncle Eddie have just retired; my arthritic aunt can only hobble painfully on a stick; my uncle is healthy enough, but needs Auntie Cecie to fasten his shoe laces in the morning.

Nellie and Cecie sleep together in the next bedroom to mine. I hear them whispering and farting as they settle down. A surly wind rattles my window. The first morning sound is of Auntie Cecie scurrying around, emptying chamber pots. She will keep on scurrying all day; and as if she hasn't enough to do in the house she scuttles to neighbours with buns or pasties, feeding the old and crippled.

Gradually, as the months pass, I settle. My parents buy Gerald, my cousin, a tennis racket, and we tread the grass courts at Perranporth. Also I become an obsessed snooker player at the Institute, where Uncle Eddie presides. Calm, courteous, quietly humorous, he is the unofficial *seigneur* of Carnkie. By day he sits in the dining room bay window, smoking a pipe, gazing out at the fields, or reading. He enjoys the *Reader's Digest* and non-fiction. He doesn't like fiction because it never happened. Now and then he will stroll to the drawing room and practise my father's songs at the piano. I'm very fond of my idle uncle.

We gather round the piano on Sunday evenings after chapel, as in my childhood. Sometimes my uncle and aunt from Redruth will join us; and perhaps my father's cousins, fine tenors. They have been 'trained', it is said; and my uncle goes for highbrow stuff, oratorio. But really it's the simple songs that we like.

> Eddie, hovering, searching for one last loud
> Chord, closing his eyes in bliss,
> Hearing it fade in my father's soulful ending.
> Leslie unveiling his score, a touch of class,
> A refining fire, to his wife's ivory smile
> Like a mild orgasm. Finger to lowered brow,
> Retired Eddie's expressionless wink
>
> At whoever caught his expression.
> Cecie scuttling out to make the tea.
> Nellie's 'Wonderful music', with a request
> For 'Wanting You'. Eddie re-installed. Soaring

My mother as my father plunged. And plunged
As his carrot-haired cousin like a seraph soared
In 'Watchman, what of the Night?':

Virginal middle-aged Owen, whose wild eyes
Conveyed the same amazement, whether he
    prayed
His beloved to come to his arms, in 'Nirvana',
'As the river flows to the ocean',
Or laughed at his own jokes without a sound.
Ethel deaf. None of them, thank God,
For Nirvana this time around.

(from Under Carn Brea)

It is a tranquil house; no one ever interferes with me. Even school becomes pleasant, as I enter the Sixth Form and am no longer forced to do cross-country runs. I have free time in which to discover Keats, Shelley, Swinburne. In summer holidays I can take them to Carn Brea, and lounge dreaming amid rock and bracken. Sexual desire is sublimated in romantic poetry, hammered away on the snooker table or tennis court.

But it surfaces with overwhelming power one Saturday afternoon at the cinema in Camborne. A girl's cheap, swirling, heady perfume. My head swims. And she leans to me, asking if I have a light; tells me there's a fair on. Ah, but my mother will be expecting me off the six o'clock bus—I dare not. I arrange to see her outside the cinema the next Saturday. All week I tremble. When Saturday comes, she doesn't turn up.

There are shy, clumsy kisses in Postman's Knock at Sunday School socials. A pal at the Institute fixes up a foursome; we walk, couple by couple, all round Carn Brea one summer evening. I'm too shy to say anything. Darkness has fallen when we reach the lane near her house. It's now or never. I say to the girl, *"Baisez-moi!"* An awkward kiss. She declines to see me again.

With the awful threat of National Service approaching, mostly I'm content to be nursed quietly by the life of the village, in which everyone is an 'aunt' or an 'uncle'. At Christmas we trail from house to house, it seems for weeks. At home, on Christmas Day, Auntie Nellie secretly dresses up in a gypsy outfit, with false protruding teeth; she rings the door-bell and is admitted to sit by the fire and tell tall stories. Though we've seen and heard it many times before, she has us rocking with laughter. There is an actress in Auntie Nellie. She recites 'England is a Garden' at concert parties.

Drizzle sweeps across the village. If you can see Carn Brea, it's going to rain; if you can't see it, it's already raining. But I have learned to love it.

"It seems to me," she says, "you had entered a very conformist phase. You'd had this turbulent, emotionally rich adolescence, then suddenly you—conformed. Yet you say you were happy."

"Because of the serene atmosphere at 'St Martin's'."

"How can you possibly say that? I'd guess it was absolutely choked-up with suppressed emotions and longings. Your uncle a widower, your aunts spinsters . . ."

"But they were getting on—in their fifties."

"And you're in your fifties. Would you say you've reached a serene, contented state?"

I snigger.

She continues, keeping up the pressure: "I'd guess it was even worse when your parents moved in after coming back from America. Your aunts, still mourning the men they'd lost in the war; your grandmother, in shock because of her son's death; your grandfather, groping his daughter Cecie and running off to his organ to escape from the family. My God! I guess it exhausted your mother—and there would have been a lot of secret jealousy too, towards a well-dressed couple just back from California with a car and a little daughter. After five years of that household, your mother would have been in no state to bear *you*."

Silence falls. It must be almost time. "Oh, I had a dream about you. You were a naked Aborigine woman crouched in the desert. You said to me, 'Go walkabout.' I've started a kind of autobiography; letting my memories flow . . ."

Silence again.

"It's time."

"Thomas, say fuck."

"No, Bombardier."

"Say fuck, or you won't get a weekend pass."

"No, Bombardier, I won't say it."

"Oh, fuck it!"

Our barracks is next to Parkhurst Prison.

"The object is to kill the enemy."

Every day a letter from my father. Loving descriptions of rugby matches.

"Thomas! I'll make a soldier of you if it's the last fucking thing I do!"

A company runner appears. "Gunner Thomas to report tomorrow at JSSL Bodmin, Bombardier."

The Russian course! And in Cornwall! So there is a God in heaven!

After lights out I'm pulled from my bed, my pyjama trousers yanked down, boot-blacking rubbed into my genitals.

Crossing Frontiers

Around the time of my return visit to Australia I was often in flight. I had no sense of gravity. The most memorable flight was the first of two trips to America for Pocket Books, to compensate them for my screwed-up semester.

My rednecked American neighbour in Executive Class was drinking heavily. He drew me into an unwanted conversation, telling me he was the New York sales manager for Rolls Royce. They'd had a bad year; he'd been summoned to England to receive a rocketing. What line, he asked, was I in? I told him I was a writer, I wrote fiction. Ah, he said, his wife liked reading fiction, but he didn't get much time for it. I showed him my novel, one of the five different covers Pocket Books were using—a girl with flaming hair.

Buying me a drink, he asked how I would be travelling around New York. By cab, I supposed. Nonsense, he said: I could have the use of one of their limos, with a chauffeur. I warmed to the man. "Really?"

"Of course. Those bums just sit on their asses all day; they might as well be sitting outside your hotel waiting for you. No problem. Call me in my office tomorrow. I'll be there at eight; I'll have it fixed for you." He gave me his card. And where else was I going to be, besides New York? Dallas and Houston. Well, he couldn't remember if they had an office in Houston, but he could certainly fix it for Dallas.

I asked if he had anything to do with Concorde. Indirectly, said the redneck; why did I ask? I said I wouldn't mind a flight on it, say at my next trip over. Since we were both selling good British products, I'd just wondered if the flight could be mutually beneficial—that is, when interviewed I could say I'd flown by Concorde and enjoyed it: assuming I had. Why, that was a great idea, he enthused; and he could surely fix it. Both ways.

"No, I'd be quite happy with one flight."

But he wouldn't hear of that. Both ways. And while we were talking, how about me sponsoring Rolls Royce for a year in return for a car?

"You really think they'd agree?" I asked, incredulous and incredibly high.

"I don't see why not. And get some money for it too."

"Oh, I wouldn't want that. A free Rolls would be enough."

"Don't undersell yourself, get some money too. Burt Lancaster does." He added a note of caution: "Mind you, I can't promise that. I'll have to talk to my boss in England. The rest—the limo, the Concorde trips—I can arrange in the office in the morning; the sponsoring decisions are made higher up, you understand. But I can't see my boss turning it down—no sirree! I think he's going to be delighted. Boy oh boy, am I glad we sat together!"

On my fourth vodka, I echoed his pleasure. I insisted on giving him a paperback; he asked me to sign it for Linda, his wife.

Our ways parted at the separate passport controls. I promised to call his office first thing in the morning. Tired and dreading a long queue for a cab, I found myself grabbed outside the terminal. "You want a cab?" I sank into the back seat. My luck was really in today. A couple of miles out of Kennedy, the driver told me the charge would be ninety dollars. I knew I'd been taken literally for a ride, but I was too exhausted to object. Besides, Pocket Books would pay. Over the car radio a suave voice, as if advertising toilet paper, urged: "Experience *The White Hotel*!"

"Hey, that's my book!" I chuckled.

"You don't say!"

I gave him a ten-dollar tip and asked for a receipt. He signed it 'Rock'.

When I awoke in the plush hotel I dialled the number on the card and asked to speak to Mr Hughes. "Mr Hughes is in England," said the secretarial voice.

"He *was* in England," I corrected her. "I flew back with him last night."

She sounded surprised. "Oh, really? We're not expecting him back in the office till Monday."

After a further confused exchange I rang off, irritated. I used cabs, happily enough, for a couple of days, then flew off to Texas, leaving the Pocket Books publicity director to get hold of Mr Hughes on Monday morning and ask him what the hell was going on.

Returning from the city of JR, I rang the publicity lady. "I called your Mr Hughes," she said, "and got an impeccably English voice. He's an ex-Guards officer. He didn't know anything about your deal. Apparently he exchanged cards in England with your redneck friend."

Once the truth had sunk in, I roared with laughter. I had told this guy I wrote fiction, and he had created one! But who was this mysterious Walter Mitty who had claimed to be an *unsuccessful* salesman! What was his motive, what did he get out of it—apart from a paperback, signed for his wife, which I had pressed on him? I never found out. But he provided me with the best fun of the trip. I didn't really want the use of a limo, a Concorde flight, or a Rolls. The reality would have been dull compared with my brush with the brilliant *improvisatore*.

He and the phoney cabman might have been seen as a warning from the Muse that I shouldn't get carried away by the hype; but truly they weren't necessary. I made up my mind from the start it was just tinsel, and resolved to enjoy it as such. I felt as much amusement as vanity in watching wallfuls of paperbacks being raided by shoppers as if they were cans of beans. I had my quiet Hereford study, the blank page in the typewriter, and my two down-to-earth households, to bring me back to what was real.

Visits to European cities were usually only for a couple of days, and I saw little apart from the airport and a hotel. In Denmark, feeling fluish, I was treated to a succession of promotional conferences and *smorgasbords*. I grew faint with hunger for real food. At the end of the two days, when my kindly hosts asked me if there was anything I'd like to do, I took them aback by snarling, "Have a hot meal." We trailed through Copenhagen in search.

The Danes were genial, the Swedes gloomy and depressed because they had nothing to be gloomy and depressed about. An intense and bluestocking blonde interviewer assured me she knew if I was telling the truth by whether my eyes shifted right or left; then disconcerted me further by saying, "Of course Lisa is you—your psyche."

An enthusiastic Breton scholar in Paris told me my novels were Celtic. I liked eroticism and the feminine, confused the borders between fantasy and reality, life and death.

I said to both, "You're right. It hadn't occurred to me."

In Amsterdam, fluish again, I embarrassed my friendly hosts by asking them to point out the red-light district on the city map. Like Freud's in a new city, my steps always turned back to the red-light district. My hosts didn't know where it was; I had to hunt for it on my own, and never found it.

I found it in Hamburg. I was on a short British Council tour with Charles Causley. We were escorted through the bright lights and harlotry of the Reeperbahn; gazed through shop windows at whores sitting in calm Rembrandt interiors, but never thought to buy. Literature and depravity aren't supposed to mix. The next afternoon, however, while Causley took a rest, I set off on my own. I was lured into a bar offering live sex for the price of a beer. The couple copulated uninterestedly a few feet from my table. Swiftly I was joined by an ugly 'hostess', who asked for champagne and fondled my thigh.

"One glass," I insisted, alarmed by the situation.

While I was still struggling with a murky menu in German I found we both had beer, schnapps and an open bottle of 'champagne' in front of us.

"You like to come upstairs?"

"*Nein, danke.* In fact, I have to go. *Ich muss* give a lecture." I demanded my bill. For a sip of schnapps I found I was having to pay the equivalent of £140. I argued; sinister shadows gathered. "You pay half," the hostess suggested. I paid it.

At the British Council office I pretended I'd been mugged. I had, in a way. They loaned me some money.

Causley and I were driven by a German friend of his to the border at Gudow. We gazed across the barbed wire at a sentry post. Birds sang in the sinister silence. It was like another form of the glass separating us from the Hamburg prostitutes. Both of us were moved, later, to write poems about the experience. I gave mine to Surkov in *Swallow*. Through this period I was haunted by borders: between east and west, life and death, poetry and prose, and others too shadowy to see.

It was good to have company, and especially Causley's company. Fellow Cornishmen, we had been friends for years. I loved his poetry, and also his freedom from cant, his effective, laconic responses to hostile situations. 'Confuse the buggers' was one; another, which he used when we found the Council had screwed up our flight to Düsseldorf, was 'Are the guns firing?' I was in a panic at possibly missing our next engagement. "Are the guns firing, Don?" he asked. As a matelot, he had had plenty of experience of that. "No," I admitted, and laughed.

The British Council officer who welcomed me to Athens had once been a schoolmaster in Malvern. A charming man, efficient and devoted to the arts, he gave no sign of regretting his change of career. His three children were still being educated in Malvern. With his pleasant wife organising a host of hired servants, he entertained me at a lavish party in their splendid house outside the city's dust and fumes. He presented me with a shaped piece of marble cut from the quarries which had given rise to the Parthenon. I asked if he could spare me another, since I knew Denise would like one, and he obliged.

I flew north to Salonika, where I hoped to catch a glimpse of Olympus. It did not appear.

Back home, I was eating supper in front of the television one evening when a familiar face appeared. The Council officer had been shot dead in Athens. Some Arab terrorist looking for a soft target. I sorrowed for his wife and children, and for our mad world.

I took Denise and Ross on a cruise of the eastern Mediterranean. The voyage brought a ghost-echo of the adolescent dreamtime; and an occurrence on the road to Ephesus convinced me that time doesn't run in a straight line. After rich but exhausting trips to Tutankhamen's treasures, the pyramids and sphinx, and Jerusalem, we almost backed out of going to Ephesus. I would have missed a cultured Turkish guide pointing to a mountain and relating the story of seven Ephesian youths who were entombed in a cave, fell asleep, and were found alive two centuries later. My heart churned; I remembered the potent, incomprehensible verses spoken voice-over in a Melbourne cinema.

> I wonder, by my troth, what thou and I
> Did, till we loved; were we not weaned till then,
> But sucked on country-pleasures, childishly?
> Or snorted we in the seven sleepers' den?

I had thought, with wonder, So this is poetry! So this is love! When, years later, I discovered the lines were from Donne's *The Good Morrow*, I never imagined I would one day see the mountain holding the seven sleepers' den. I glimpsed, not for the first time, some mysterious pattern beneath the chaos of experience.

I went further east, to Bulgaria, on an official trip for the British Council. I was the first author to go there following the appearance of Malcolm Bradbury's *Rates of Exchange*, in which the hero is advised by a refined Council lady on no account to commit buggery. I would be safe, I knew, from that temptation, but Slaka-Bulgaria sounded hazardous. A refined lady advised me on no account to mention Bradbury's novel.

Arriving at Sofia's airport I was welcomed by a nervous Embassy official, a suave official of the Writers' Union, and a pale gaunt blonde who said, "Mr Thomas, I will be your guardian angel."

Her name was Nelli. And she did truly become my guardian angel. Staying with me each evening for a week, far beyond her hours of duty, she saved me not only from buggery but from every possible sexual temptation. She made sure I ate as well as anyone in Sofia can do. Women's Week was on; the restaurants were packed with factory parties, men thanking women for being their slaves the rest of the year, Nelli explained. A fervent Communist, a Komsomol leader, she stormed at headwaiters to find us a table; and if anger failed to work she resorted shamelessly to tears. Always we got a table. She was the only woman I've met who smoked more than I: pausing to smoke, not merely between courses but between mouthfuls. Her face and hands trembled constantly with nerves, as though beneath her pale taut skin was a swarm of bees. We argued all day about Communism, and I came to rely on her like a mother.

Sunk deep in a leather sofa at the Writers' Union headquarters, liberally plied with brandy, I listened to a rugged grey-haired Secretary declaim on the need for writers to band together in the interests of the proletariat. I reminded him that his country's first poet was Orpheus, who banded with no one except stones and trees. The Union boss said every writer had complete freedom in Bulgaria; indeed there was a well-known so-called dissident who had toured Australia: perhaps I'd heard of him? I said no, but I would like to meet him. Of course: no problem: it would be arranged.

But when the evening came for my meeting with the well-known dissident, unfortunately he fell sick.

Still, the amount of western literature published in Bulgaria was impressive. With Nelli as my shadow, I sat in an office of the largest publishers of foreign literature, conversing with three stiff-backed ladies in black who looked like the three Fates. Gesturing towards shelves full of English fiction, they handed me their latest Fay Weldon. But their problem, they said severely, was that my country produced so few novels that were worth translating. I agreed. Nelli looked upset; the three Fates hadn't even acknowledged that my own work existed.

I enquired about Soviet literature: for instance, Pasternak. Yes, they had published translations of almost all his work. *Doctor Zhivago*? No, not that one, because it was rather poor.

"That may be so," I said. "But are you telling me that a

good novel by Fay Weldon is more worthy of publication than a bad novel by Pasternak, who is a great genius?"

Three shrugs. "Perhaps not. But just because he is a genius we think it would be unfair to him to let our people read such a poor novel."

I took my leave, rather abruptly. Outside, Nelli raged against their rudeness. It didn't matter, I assured her. It was our last evening together; she wanted to take me to the best hotel-restaurant in Sofia. Again it was full; again she stormed and, when that failed, wept. The waiters made us up a little table almost touching the piano. To the thunder of a jazz pianist in roll-necked sweater we drank and smoked and chatted sentimentally. It had been fun, we agreed.

The pianist glided into a selection from Hollywood films and Broadway. I murmured, "Play it again, Sam!" and with a smile Sam swung into the theme from *Casablanca*. Leaning across, I crooned, assured her that a kiss was just a kiss. Nelli, flushed, confused, dragged nervously at her cigarette.

"Come up for a nightcap," I begged her.

"No, I must go home."

Politely we shook hands.

Next morning at the airport, just as I was moving into passport control, she pushed past the suave Writers' Union official, threw herself into my arms, giving me a passionate kiss. "I've been so silly!" she gasped. "Come back! Please come back!"

She knew I would never come back. Or if I did, she or I would no longer be the same. Such passionate embraces are for passport control.

Whether I was appearing in England or abroad, I confronted astonishing extremes of response to my work. Without seeking or wishing to be controversial, it seemed I couldn't avoid it. In Frankfurt, an English member of the audience went into a paroxysm of anger over a scene in *The Flute-Player* in which Elena is raped in a bath by an old janitor. I tried to point out to him that the style was parodic and the incident echoed the myth of Leda and the Swan. In the same audience two thin-lipped women attacked me over the beginning of *Ararat*, which I had read. "Sergei Rozanov had made an unnecessary journey from Moscow to Gorky, simply in order to sleep with a young blind woman . . ." Why, the women demanded, had I named Rozanov but not, for some time, the blind woman? It was a clear case of chauvinism. My response, that I was exposing Rozanov's lack of interest in her as a person, carried no weight with them. I saw them, and others, as being so blinded by their ideology that they could pay no attention to the subtlety of a literary text.

And the English, in particular, felt that sex could be treated from a cool, ironic distance, but should not carry any suggestion of the numinous, as it does in Yeats, Joyce, Dylan Thomas, and earlier Celtic writers and storytellers. In *The White Hotel*, which continued to arouse the most passionate feeling for or against, many readers who found the eroticism acceptable or even highly enjoyable expressed doubts about the last section's religious metaphor. Some thought I was describing heaven, having no concept of purgatory.

A rabbi and a Catholic schoolmaster wrote to say they were recommending the book to their flocks; yet supposedly liberal and radical readers often found it pornographic and disgusting. The criticism mostly centred on the violence done to Lisa. I found this difficult to comprehend. Lisa was a victim (with other women, men, and children) of a holocaust which was created by men: I was reflecting history. My heroine was incomparably the most sympathetic human being in the novel; I could say—as the Swedish interviewer recognised—'*Lisa Erdman—c'est moi.*' Ironically, while I was being accused of hostility to women, I myself was troubled by a different problem: how to create male characters as sympathetic as my female characters.

Of course I recognised that my work might not be without disturbing undertones; simply because I, like every one of my readers, was not without sin, not without shadows. This was in part what *The White Hotel* was about: that we were all involved in the evil, we could not pretend it was outside us.

I needed my trips away, because while I was at home I could think of nothing else but the page I was working on—and the next blank page. I tried to relax, at Denise's each evening, but secretly I was glad when the hour came for me to say good-bye and, driving home, withdraw into my imagination. 'Home' and 'imagination' were almost synonyms. There is a lovely Cornish dialect word, 'home-along': homeward-bound. Whether I was in Finland or on Paddington station or spending an evening with a friend in Hereford, I always welcomed the moment when I could go home-along. I recognised it as a need, stemming perhaps from insecurity, which goes back to my childhood. When I lived at 'Beverly', and again in the flat at Melbourne, I enjoyed going home. It was where I could be calm, where I could be creative.

I liked turning into the drive at Greyfriars; and, though I might give only a cursory greeting to my wife and children —and sometimes none at all—before going to my study, I felt their reassuring presence. Especially I needed Maureen's quiet strength, and her certainty that what I was doing was valuable. She didn't make the mistake of thinking that when I was quiet, when I appeared to be idling, I necessarily *was* idle. Creative herself in a practical way, she was extraordinarily sensitive to my creative moods. That made her for me a kind of talisman.

Entering my silent study in the late evening, my nape prickled. There was the waiting page in the typewriter, saying, "Why have you been so long?" Around me were my creative ikons. A portrait of Akhmatova, stern-faced in the early Soviet style. Pushkin lounging poetically on a bench at Tsarskoye Selo, a cheap memento of my Leningrad trip. Virgin and Child, a silver replica of a bronze Donatello roundel. My radiant dark-haired mother, cradling my sister —or it might be me; it didn't seem to matter which.

Framed, my Uncle Willie's plans of the underground levels of a Colombian silver mine. A black-and-white photograph of the Botallack engine house, set against the sea. Another large framed photo taken in 1903 from the summit of Carn Brea; ancient stone circle in the foreground, Carnkie with its smok-ing tin mines in the distance. The unknown photographer has caught 'St Martin's'; it's strange to think that my father is inside that tiny white house, three years old. Is he playing?

eating? being dressed or bathed? What images flash for him?

Some two years older, he stands between his parents' chairs in a family group, taken in front of the house. My grandfather is wide-moustached, a watch chain dangling from his waist-coat; my grandmother looks austere, resigned. Lightly her hand supports Leslie, aged about two, in a dress. Thin-faced Nellie squats on her other side; the older children, unsmiling in the moment's solemnity, stand clustered. Great-aunt Martin, black-gowned, sharp-nosed, sits facing aside stubbornly, in widowed isolation, as if to say she doesn't belong. Donald, the youngest, who gave me my name, is not yet born.

Whenever I visited Cornwall on holiday, for some reason I avoided Carnkie and the environment of my youth. Well, one reason was obvious: I had with me a woman they wouldn't have recognised. Yet they wouldn't have known me either. To the ageing villagers, my 'aunts' and 'uncles', I was Donald; they didn't know the unquiet Don. Taking the new motor-way, I'd glance left at Carn Brea, knowing it as the centre of my being; yet I breathed more freely when it was past.

Though Denise kept urging me, I rarely took flowers to my parents' grave; it grieved me too much. The stone, with its lines from Shelley, was stained, and the plot overgrown with weeds.

I did once visit the Carnkie Count House, having heard it had been turned into a good restaurant. Its walls were dec-orated with photographs of pale-faced subterranean miners. My prawn cocktail cost more than my ancestors, lining up there, would have received for a week's toil. I didn't enjoy my meal.

Nice

I was mining *Sphinx*, as my ancestors mined Carn Brea, or the silver mines of Colombia. There were so many problems, so little reward, that I almost believed the seam was exhausted. Just as I had feared, I was lost in a labyrinth. Yet writing is always like 'tributing', working 'this week for nothing, next for fifty pounds'. Three times Andrew Hewson, my literary agent, courageously sent the novel back to me as unfinished.

Maureen returned from a holiday with a new man-friend. They had stayed at a converted granite cottage I had bought in Cornwall. After she had cooked me some scrambled eggs, she told me quietly they had decided to get married. I felt momentary relief, then panic.

"When?"

"In a few months."

"So soon? Well, make your plans, but just don't tell me. I've got to finish my novel, and I need calm."

Calm rather than ecstasy was the essential requisite for inspiration, Pushkin observed. But I could be no calmer, faced with this coming revolution, than was Pushkin when he loaded his pistol for the fatal duel.

Thrusting away the uncertain future, I wrote on. The novel had fallen, over a period of two years, into three separate *genres*: drama, prose narrative, and verse. A kind of troika, apt for the third book of a sequence. I thought it was a strained, though intriguing, form. As a few thoughtful critics would observe, I crammed in too much material; but I seemed to lack both the calm and the skill to fine it down. An excess of invention was at least better than not enough. While *Ararat* and *Swallow* had received similar, mixed reactions in England and America, *Sphinx* would be generally dispraised by English critics for being too clever, praised by Americans for being imaginative.

Struggling to get it finished in time, I poured my negative emotions into Lloyd George, a Welsh journalist visiting Leningrad. I caused him to be led a dance by a woman of majestic mien whom I had seen in the Nikol'sky Cathedral and dreamed of approaching. George's background was similar to mine: a Celtic mining family, first-generation University, marital upheavals; but I felt superior to him because his people had been hemmed by narrow horizons, and he hadn't had my Dreamtime experience. What might have been a creative imagination had turned to political radicalism and rancour. He had not had the luck to gaze at the terrible tree, to suck at Sheba's Breasts.

I decided to make him go crazy. And Rozanov, that familiar from the two previous novels, quits the madness of his muddled amours for a *psikhushka*, a penal psychiatric institution.

I hadn't intended to write a trilogy, a troika—or as it turned out, a quartet. I had regarded *Ararat* as a work on its own; but on the very last page, when the storyteller Rozanov goes to his study at midnight to work, it seemed to open out; and seemed also to invite me, the author, into the fiction.

When *Ararat* was published, hostile reviewers wrote of its pornography and chauvinism. I asked myself, What would they have said if a woman had written it? Surely, that she had written a biting portrayal of male attitudes. Yet the text would have been the same.

I conceived the idea of 'giving' my *Ararat* text to an Italian *improvisatrice*, performing in Finland, and of having it discussed by a panel of judges. Encircling that fictional group of critics would be another panel of judges, the reviewers and readers of *Swallow*. I wished to throw into question the concepts of a 'pure' text, divorced from its author, and of objective criticism. A creative writer may pretend he is floating on a calm sea, but in reality he is storm-tossed, maybe sinking. A critic always pretends he is sitting calmly on the shore; but in reality he carries his own storm inside his head.

Once I was engaged on my unorthodox sequel to *Ararat*, I guessed a third novel was inevitable. Two is no number in literature. The novels were improvisational because I didn't know from day to day, page to page, what would emerge. Within a volume I could do what I liked with my characters, limited only by what I had established of their lives in a previous volume. In that respect my way of writing resembled life, my own or anyone's. Tension between freedom and restraint led to problems as the sequence emerged. For ex-ample, in *Swallow* I decided the young wife of my travelling poet Surkov should be the daughter of his neighbour and *alter ego*, Rozanov. But a single sentence in *Ararat*, as I belatedly discovered, made this impossible; or at least, she would have had to become Surkov's mistress at the age of eight. I knew Dante had fallen in love with an eight-year-old, but he hadn't made Beatrice his mistress. I toyed with making Surkov a paedophile; however, I eventually gave the paedophilia to a Soviet editor in *Sphinx*.

I grew oppressed with a thousand pages of rough abandoned sheets, stuffed with unlived events.

The monster resisted ordering, controlling, just as my life did. Life and art were too close, like *Titanic* and iceberg.

Insofar as I was able to be rational about my intentions, I felt I was struggling to achieve an inclusive form: one that would allow me to switch easily from fantasy to reality and back, from fiction to poetry to drama to autobiography—anything I felt like. Poetry leaps over startling abysses from one image to the next; cinema goers readily accept and understand a collage treatment; why should the boring old novel be any different? Doesn't the novel reader want to be taken by surprise?

Everything had gone wrong in the Oblonsky household. The common-law wife, formerly the legal wife, had started seeing a divorced man and had announced that she was going to marry him. The marriage had taken place three weeks ago, and her departure was having a distressing effect on her ex-husband. He would spend much of his time wandering aimlessly from empty room to room, or pacing the garden, which was piled with damp autumnal leaves. He would search in vain for humble domestic articles, such as waste-disposal sacks or string. He kept noting familiar coffee tables or pictures that had disappeared. The daily callers, who had always been happy to drink his coffee or sherry, no longer called; they were calling instead on the newly married couple to offer congratulations. Oblonsky, they felt, deserved what he was getting, for he had been unfaithful and driven his wife to this action. So whereas, in Tolstoy's novel, it was the departing woman who was ostracised, in these more enlightened times it was her former partner from whom they turned away. When a pin-ball machine is tilted, all the little rusty balls run to one side. It was the same in this case.

On the third weekend after the marriage Stepan Arkadyevich Oblonsky—Stiva, as he was generally called by his friends—awoke at his usual time, which was about eight o'clock. He turned his plump, pampered body over on the springs, as if he had a mind for a long sleep, and hugged the pillow, pressing his cheek to it.

He distinctly heard his wife's voice call 'Stiva' from the foot of the stairs, the daily signal that she had set down a tray of toast and tea for him to fetch. It was not quite such an indulgence as it sounds, since Stiva always worked until well past midnight whereas Dolly went to bed early and rose early. "Just a few more moments," he thought, "and then I'll get the tray. Tea, toast and the first cigarette—how wonderful!"

He opened his eyes in the curtained bedroom, and saw a lamp still shining. "Oh my God, the house is empty!" he thought. From his youth, if Oblonsky was in an empty house at night, he had found it necessary to have a light burning. He went over all the details of their last moments together: the large cheque for her he had written in his study; the list of useful telephone numbers (including her own) she had given him in exchange; the gaggle of women friends who came to help her pack crockery; his agitated tears, the peck on his cheek before he drove off, unwilling to face the days of packing.

"And the worst of it is that I am to blame for everything—I am to blame and yet I am not to blame."

He swung his legs off the bed, stood—swaying slightly —and reached for his red dressing gown. After peeing and washing his hands, he padded downstairs. Reaching the cold kitchen lino he felt his left foot tread on something soft; he saw it was shit left by one of the cats, who were beginning to feel disturbed. He cursed. He wiped his foot with a dish-towel, then filled the kettle.

"But what is to be done? What can I do?" he asked himself despairingly.

He took a sliced loaf from the bread bin. The two pieces he slotted in the toaster felt stale. He would have to buy fresh. There was always something one had to buy. He wasn't used to living alone.

He had dropped a bag of pears at the supermarket while fumbling for money. One of his neighbours happened to be queueing behind him, and she had given him an amused though compassionate look.

After eating breakfast and feeding the cats, Oblonsky dressed and went to his study to work. But, with the silent house accusing him, he couldn't concentrate. Before, he had loved his study; now he was beginning to hate it. It was a useless appendix to his prison.

All he could do was hammer away at the keys, relentlessly, not bothering to think. Because he felt so depressed, he was writing a farce. Oblonsky felt he was sleep-writing, and when he woke up he would have no more to write.

I'd found a post at a mixed Grammar School in Teignmouth, not too far from home. In the summer months between Oxford and teaching, I sensed a loneliness in my father. Something had happened, but I wasn't sure what. He and my mother had been seeing a lot of a neighbour, an attractive middle-aged woman whose husband was abroad. Usually they went out as a threesome, but once my father took her to the pictures on their own. My mother didn't like the cinema.

I found my mother weeping—real sorrowful tears, not the April showers that used to cross her happy face over someone's misfortune three or four times a day. She hinted at cruel gossip. Then their friend's husband came home, with unexpected suddenness, and my parents were invited to the welcoming tea party. Father's sadness or loneliness seemed to grow after that. Maureen and I asked him to come with us to see *Carmen Jones* at the Regal. Sitting by us, he seemed alone.

My mother kept telling him, as she had done for years, that he was working too hard. His gentle face was deep-trenched, like Auden's. But he was very proud of the houses he built, and would take us to show them off. He offered to come to Teignmouth and build us a bungalow.

It was strange to think of real marriage—living together —after a year when I'd either been away or had kept my base firmly at 'St Martin's'. We found a flat at Dawlish, a short train ride along the coast. When we moved in, she was too busy making the flat right, and I in coping with my first job, to wonder whether we had a good marriage.

School was at first a nightmare. It was a pleasant, small country school, with decent children, but I couldn't keep order. Every lesson was warfare, and I antagonised the good children by keeping them in along with the bad. If I put a small group in detention they were often unruly, busty girls. I was discovering the lion in the corner of the classroom; and losing some of my shyness. Anyway, you could hardly avoid treating the girls more personally when you were expected to call them by their Christian names, the boys by their surnames —an absurd hangover, like the separate staffrooms, from segregated days.

My evenings were packed with marking and preparation. On Saturdays Maureen and I treated ourselves to a trip to Exeter to see a film. On the way back to the station I would sometimes make an excuse to detour alone through the market, to pick up a secret copy of *Spick* or *Span*.

One Saturday we saw *Psycho*. The large detached house in

which we lived stood on a hill, and as we approached it on that moonlit night it became the psychotic house of the film. We clung together; and afterwards laughed shakily.

A milder shock was the news that my father had to go into hospital for a prostate operation, just before Christmas. It would be routine, but messy and involving a slow recuperation. When we arrived at the home of Maureen's parents for the Christmas holidays, her mother shocked me by saying he was in a bad way, having haemorrhaged after the operation. At 'St Martin's' my mother, though looking anxious, assured us he had pulled out of it. I was angry with my mother-in-law for having alarmed me unnecessarily. On his leaving 'St Martin's', Mother said, he had stared back at it as if he would never see it again. Worse—he had bought her an electric blanket.

When we visited him, he looked gaunt and weak. Still, he was able to chat with us and smile. The surgeon had assured him the operation would be like 'a smash-and-grab raid' —unpleasant but not dangerous; yet the treatment of his haemorrhage, a tube thrust up his penis, had been agony. The pale, sweat-streaked face propped on pillows glanced towards the end of the ward, by the door; "I've seen five go," he said.

"Go?"

He smiled ironically. "To the happy hunting grounds! They wheel their bed down to the end, so they can be removed without too much upset. And I've seen Tojo. He comes and takes a look around."

Tojo's task was to shave the corpses, for which he would get half-a-crown. Maureen and I had a friend who nursed at the hospital; she had told us, months before, a droll story—how Tojo had marked down a patient as in the last stages, then 'lo and behold, the bugger hupped and revived!' I had told my father and he'd had a good laugh. Now I regretted telling him.

He improved a little over Christmas, which for us was subdued and dispirited. Each evening a neighbour, Willie, drove my mother and others in the family to the hospital. While his body stayed weak his spirit was returning. He sang "Mary's Boy Child" to his fellow sufferers, and said he spent a lot of time gazing through a window at a distant view of Basset Carn, thinking he only wanted to get out and enjoy life, enjoy singing. Essentially, we knew, he was strong; he had told the surgeon on arrival that he felt strong enough to tear the hospital down with his bare hands. I wish he had done so.

He told my mother he kept showing her photo around and telling everyone what a wonderful wife she was: almost as though he had had to discover it anew in this crisis. He also said to her that if anything should happen to him he wanted her to know "my way is clear". "That's wonderful, dear!" she said.

She could relate that quite cheerfully because at the New Year he had a remarkable improvement. Mother came home radiant from an afternoon visit: he felt so much better he was out of bed and helping to push the food trolleys around! We rejoiced, and relaxed into festivity for the first time. That evening, he still felt pretty good though he had a slight temperature.

The temperature wouldn't go back to normal. On my last day I called to see him outside of visiting-hours. I found him sitting out of bed reading the *News Chronicle*, but he didn't seem 'with me'. I went back to Devon and teaching, deeply worried.

On the following Sunday afternoon, while I was marking some books, the owner of our flat knocked to say there was a phone call for me. It was Uncle Leslie, his deep voice breaking: I must come home. I flung myself sobbing on my bed, and Maureen tried to comfort me. She packed my dark suit. We caught the train.

Uncle Leslie was waiting for us at Redruth station. I was driven in a state of madness to the hospital. The noise of the garish ward, with a Salvation Army band singing a hymn, burst on me; there were screens round a bed by the door and my father lay, tossing in agony, his pyjama coat open, his body bathed in sweat all over. My mother said in a crooning, anguished, exalted voice, "Look dear, Donald has come!" I hung back, shy even now of touching him. "Give Dad a hug," she told me, and I embraced him.

She and I stayed with him all night. She was frightened when nurses put an oxygen tube in his nose, but they reassured her it was to help him breathe. A stroke had led to pneumonia; he was fighting for every rasping breath. With the oxygen and the approach of dawn he appeared quieter, and Mother felt hopeful enough to ask if they could give him some coffee, 'to build up his strength'. They probably didn't; they asked us to leave for a few minutes and we rested in a night room. My mother told me that she'd been woken three nights ago by a nun standing in the bedroom doorway: she had said, "Only three days more, then you will be sleeping alone."

We went back to him, back to the get well cards and the groaning fruit bowl. He was tossing and rasping again. Mother sat and clutched his hand and prayed.

When she left to go to the toilet I took his hand and said to him, "I love you. I've always loved you." It was the first time I had ever said it. I know he heard me, although he gave no sign; all night he had not spoken. Desperately willing him to live, I said, lying, "Maureen is pregnant—we're going to have a baby!"

He shaped his mouth with a huge effort to say, indistinctly, "Nice!"

Mother came back; soon after, a male nurse. He checked my father's pulse; said nonchalantly, "Ten minutes," and walked away. Wandering blindly into the corridor, I met Willie, come to see if we needed a lift home. "He's dying!" I cried, and Willie, white-faced, gasped: "Sure 'nuff?"

"Yes!" I leaned my head against a wall and sobbed.

Outside, night was fading into a late iron-grey January dawn. I leaned against a window pane. Across from me was another wing, its windows lit. A young nurse stood framed in one of them, brushing long black hair unhurriedly. For her, a dull routine day was beginning. His breaths, when I returned to the screened bed, were widely spaced. "Take his hand, dear." We sat one on either side, clasping him. She started to whisper the Lord's Prayer, and I joined in. There was an interval between breaths which seemed impossibly long; yet one more breath was dragged from his lungs. Then stillness again.

Imperceptible, the change from life to death. Yet there was no mistaking its majesty, its awe, its horror.

Willie drove us home. The house filled with wails. Mother insisted I must eat, and fried bacon, sausage and egg. A boy delivered his *News Chronicle*. I couldn't conceive how the world could be continuing. A postman delivered the familiar yellow envelope of the *National Geographic*. I went back to the ward to pick up his personal effects. His pyjamas had been laundered, but in the breast-pocket I found a white handker-chief, screwed up and wringing with his sweat. Three or four more get well cards had arrived.

The village drew its blinds. A roof of cloud hung, and the day never truly broke. People called in and cried with us. Mother's doctor offered her a sleeping pill but she refused it saying, "I might never wake up!" It consoled and a little surprised me that she wanted to wake up. We decided to sleep that night in the one bed—Mother, Maureen and I. Leaving my mother to clear up, as she insisted, Maureen and I went to bed, and I entered her fiercely, determined to turn my white lie into truth. Mother came up and undressed in the dark, her corset metals jingling. We giggled as we crowded up.

I caught a bus to Camborne to register his death, and overheard a woman say to her companion, "Did you hear Harold Thomas is dead?" I was angry; his brimming life had turned to a small interesting item of gossip. Besides, the world had died, not my father; the two women were dead but they didn't know it. In the afternoon the coffin was brought home, to a wailing of aunts, and laid in the drawing room. I looked at the wax face, but he wasn't there.

I seemed to be floating as I followed him into the chapel. "I am the Resurrection and the life" buoyed me up higher and I couldn't feel the ground. I sang the hymns loudly, with harmonies; afterwards Gerald touched my arm and said gruffly, "You were very brave."

I went back to school a week after his death. I dreaded 9.25, the moment when he died. My 'O' level class, who normally played me up as much as anyone, was hushed in sympathy. I couldn't stand the unnatural strain, and at 9.25 I cracked a joke. My pupils let out a secret sigh of relief, and started catcalling and joking.

SEVENTEEN

Floods

Maureen was pregnant. Her belly was huge as I started my second year of teaching. All my classes were different except one. With the new classes I could keep control, but the class I hadn't got rid of still created bedlam. They were to carry on following and harrying me, from the Second to the Fifth form, and remained untameable.

I loved my pupils, especially the girls, with a fierce hate, hated them with a fierce love. I wrote about my feelings;

> Maiden and harlot
> ('Has made little progress')
> Our breath is taken by
> Your insolent escalations
> Between two summers.
> Schoolgirl, where are you?
> Here—no here.
> So candid, clandestine,
> Gymslip to white blouse and tie,
> You've put on breasts and hairstyles,
> And, remote at the back
> —Last year on grass neuter—
> Dim traces of eye-shadow
> On secretive sex-haunted eyes.
> (While we, wearing leather
> Patches on elbows, sit a chair nearer
> Our stately Superego.)

Sue, Lyn, Loraine, Katrina—stop!
My false-loves, why rush away,
And where do you think you're heading? Keep calm;
Maturity's a date that can wait; he isn't

Likely to stand you up, so make *him* hang
Around, keep him uncertain. He'll have you soon

    Enough in his close, seductive car to take you
    To whatever technique and lay-by he's selected.
    Be less eager, don't fall completely for
    His blind embrace which screws by averages.
    I'd like to guess your desolate destinations
    By reading your grouped faces; but can only
        warn—
    'Don't trust maturity'; swing your satchels still,
    And stay like cherries on my snakeless tree.

    I know I shall never know such love again
    As this. The gentle coition of my fingers
    On fingers, correcting, improving; or of breasts
    Unaware of themselves, against gown; or in
        corridor
    A girl climbing some steps in front of me, turning
        With pepsodent grin at my words, her short skirt
    Cheekily flaring away from upstraining
        stockings—
    Their ladders stretching Jacob-like to heaven;
    The indecent jokes they tell me;
        desk-arraignments—
    'Hazel Priest is a pro, she charges 7/6';
    Hazel herself tender as I story-tell
    About Rikki-Tikki-Tavi or Man-Shy,
    So that I feel a blinding love for her.
Yet when they escalate out of this panorama,
Jostling with duffle-bags through Eden's exit,
They're in such a hurry to meet real life
They probably don't say cheerio (nothing has
    happened),
But leave me like an angel to clear up
The torn pin-ups, record sleeves, combs, love notes,
    tampaxes,
And are henceforth shadows on this photograph.
        (On Looking at the Latest School Panoramic Photo)

Almost as immature as those girls, the poems were the first I wrote which had some sense of individuality. It wasn't quite true that nothing had happened. I'd fallen for a big-thighed, cheerful Fifth-former, and had enjoyed a snatched kiss or two at school parties.

Christmas came. We took Caitlin, three months old, home with us. We found my mother, my aunts and uncle, huddled in the dark drawing room, under the portrait of the benefactor. With croons of delight they leapt hungrily on the new soul.

The house and the village had darkened. Auntie Cecie spent a lot of time in bed, and had lost her faith. She no longer went to chapel. The choir was falling apart without my father's sweet and powerful voice. I loved Auntie Cecie almost as much as my mother, and was sad to see her so changed. My mother was struggling on, going to whist drives and bingo, but seemed a half-person.

Still, our baby warmed the house; and warmed ours in Devon. We visited Paris at Easter, but returned a day early, missing her.

I strove to overcome my grief. I hadn't cried for several months when I played a new LP of *Gerontius*. That made me burst into tears.

The second Christmas of his death was looming. I had a call from Maureen at school to say Auntie Cecie was dead. My colleagues wondered why I wept for an aunt. I couldn't get away till the weekend so Maureen went ahead, with the baby. I invited Loraine, my cheerful Fifth-former, to come to the flat after school; she had taken to calling as a baby-sitter. Grief made me lustful; she agreed to come to bed with me if she could keep her clothes on. Then—probably thinking of her skirt—she asked should she take it off. It's an image that has hardly faded: creamy flesh above her black stockings, doubled in the dressing-table mirror.

She refused to make love. For hours we lay caressing. Grief and lust wrestled together as the light faded. At long last she submitted; navy pants rasped over suspenders; but by then I was too sore.

A sexual act leaves no memories. There are no sexual madeleines. Memory doesn't give a fuck about sex. It cares only for emotions, including frustration. I recall my soreness and grief at the end of that day, whereas I have forgotten a thousand fulfilling acts of love.

I went home to a house in despair. Aunt Nellie, in a downstairs bed, had pneumonia. Uncle Eddie, during our parody of a Christmas dinner, keeled over with a mild heart-attack. My mother, with arthritis starting to cripple her hands, couldn't cope with two invalids. Maureen kept house gallantly, while I tried to chop up several dozen bundles of kindling wood in my grandfather's tool shed; but I totally lacked the family's practical bent. As Uncle Leslie once scornfully remarked: "Donald couldn't even close a door!" In any case we could only stay for a few days. I tried to persuade my reviving uncle and aunt to keep the house, we could perhaps find a family who would move in and look after them. But without Cecie, who had kept everything going single-handed, the house meant nothing. Uncle Eddie would live with his daughter-in-law's parents (Gerald had married); Auntie Nellie would have to go into a Home. I raged against the death of the house.

The family who bought it were old village neighbours, and they allowed my mother to keep our part, separating it off into a flat. That was a problem solved; but the house, the tribal house, had died. My aunt died of loneliness in the Home a year or so later. My uncle died in his son's house on the Isle of Wight, after I'd lost touch with them.

It was a sort of holocaust.

Everyone knows what he was doing when President Kennedy was shot. I was standing by the TV behind a girl who was styling Maureen's hair. The news came through; I felt sick, felt—I still do—the world would never be the same; yet I was pleased the BBC didn't cancel the succeeding comedy show because it was one that I liked. I drove the hairdresser home and we fondled in a lay-by.

It wasn't the first or the last time I have felt a peculiar contradiction between superficial response to some tragedy —which may even be excitement, stimulation—and the profound response, which may never fade.

Maureen and I had moved to Hereford with our two children: Sean had just been born. We lived not far from the Cathedral, in a quiet cul-de-sac; the Wye ran behind our overgrown garden. We soon found the sylvan Wye was prone to overflow; after a few days of rain a lorry would come round delivering sandbags and we would prepare for the siege. During one such period of rain, in 1966, the television brought news of a tragedy which affected me even more profoundly than Kennedy's assassination: a slurry-tip collapsed in the Welsh mining-village of Aberfan, forty miles away; a primary school was buried, and twenty-one adults and 116 children were killed. I wrote, with painful slowness, a Requiem for the village.

The river water would creep stealthily around our semi-detached house, lap the sandbagged front door, but usually decide not to enter. They were exciting times: we would carry what we could upstairs, prop the piano on bricks, and withdraw upstairs ourselves, armed with a primus stove and provisions. At night I would two or three times go to the bedroom window to try to gauge if the flood was still rising or had started to recede. The amber light of a streetlamp stretched across the avenue, taut as a violin string; and my breast would be just as tense. Next day, neighbours would fetch their shopping in rowing boats; everyone had a Dunkirk spirit; these were the only times when I overcame my shyness and reserve and exchanged friendly greetings with our neighbours.

The floods were good, because in the crisis, I appreciated my wife's calm efficiency and hard work; too often I took her virtues for granted. The flooded Wye brought us close together: man, woman, two children, a cat. Our normal lives were drifting apart. I was seeing other women, including our hairdresser-friend—a Welsh girl with lustrous dramatic eyes and full lips. She was sensual and religious, keeping me

hovering on the edge for a year, and even then, in the act of
love, determined to claim a certain innocence . . .

> Unsuckable tits, her teeth dropping grips,
> skirls of laughter as she combed and set
> her tutor's wife's hair, I stooped to run
> my hand up her skirt when that tremor went
> across the screen that's still not stopped—
> Kennedy shot. Expert with tongue and lips,
> she tuned me to a pitch of keening want
> beyond the range of dogs, the frequency
> of outer space, her sleek, fugitive cunt.
>
> A touch of her cool fingers was enough.
> I laughed hysterically. And she—then cried.
> Let me sleep with her only when she slept;
> Her parents away. Needed to bring me home
> to the terraces of rain, the pall of smoke,
> sad chapels. I understood. It was love
> unwove her in the night, her lashes wet.
>   (From *Big Deaths, Little Deaths*)

Around the time of Aberfan, I met a dark-haired girl called
Denise who was slim, volatile and innocent, yet with a
promise of passionate excitation. On our third or fourth secret
date she pushed away my hand, saying, "You want too much
too soon." It thrilled and disturbed me.

I published a booklet of my poetry. I had to pay for its
printing myself through promised subscriptions. Most of the
subscribers were staff or senior pupils from Teignmouth
Grammar School, and staff and students at the College in
Hereford. The publisher, Howard Sergeant, had grouped
what he believed rightly to be the best poems—erotic poems
about schoolgirls—at the front. I ought to have sensed danger
but didn't. I was hauled in front of the Education Director,
ordered to take back the copies meant for students. I was
lucky, he said—if I'd still been teaching in Devon I'd have
got the sack. The reaction from Teignmouth wasn't good.

Only the French teacher, whom I had thought a prim spinster, liked the poems. My Hereford Head of Department, a kindly conservative man, was outraged: worried that some students would refuse to have me as their tutor—and that others might try to insist on having me.

"My problem is, I lack commitment."

"No, I'd say you've had almost too much commitment."

"True."

"You've a problem with compartmentalisation," she corrects.

"Ah—yes!"

"—And with closeness. You can only get close through physical touch. You've been desperately trying to get in real touch with your mother."

"I'm not sure it's anything so personal. I think it's to do with our family myth, the Italian *improvisatore* who came and seduced my great-great-grandmother. When he abandoned her and their twin daughters, she never smiled again. So the story goes; he's not in the parish registers but I know he existed. And he set up a turbulence which carries through the generations. You think that's nonsense."

"It doesn't matter what I believe; it's why *you* should believe it . . . Anyway, it's time."

EIGHTEEN

Mazes

Shlee godi, as Pushkin wrote in a famous love poem: years passed. Life as a College lecturer was enjoyable and not onerous. The English Department had its own separate, spacious and comfortable house; my study would once have been someone's ample bedroom, and our seminar rooms were furnished with carpets and easy chairs. No wonder we believed in the civilising influence of literature. It wasn't a hardship to sit with a cigarette, discussing Yeats or Frost, in front of a dozen nubile young women. We could set our own syllabus, teach our favourite authors. It was pleasant to gossip with colleagues over a sherry and a nice lunch; pleasant to finish the short day with a few private tutorials. I tried to be fair, but inevitably gave more time to those who were attractive and intelligent. In the early 70s, as the College expanded, some scruffy, bearded male students appeared. My tutorials with them were brisk.

The lighter burden allowed me to spend more time on my poetry. I wrote, at weekends and in the vacations, at a card-table in our bedroom. It gave rise to a droll misunderstanding, as reported to us.

"Have you met Maureen Thomas? . . . She's very nice. Her husband's a poet."

"My God! Really?"

"Yes. He sits up in their bedroom."

"How awful for her!"

"Not awful. He makes quite a lot of money from it, as a matter of fact."

"Oh my God!"

"He's just published his first poetry book."

"Oh, poet! I thought you said pervert!"

I can't imagine how my wife's friend thought I made a lot of money from poetry. Occasionally I would receive a couple of pounds from a magazine. In '68 my first collection, *Two Voices*, was published, with a royalty of £100. The money, of course, was irrelevant: it was thrill enough to hold the slim book in my hands.

The cherry blossom on our garden tree bloomed and vanished, year after year; a swing appeared under it, and various footballs succeeded each other in the high grass; one grey Lucina (named after Auden's cat) died and gave way to another. (Our present Lucina is the third.) An old piano was bought, used by the children for a while, then fell silent. Maureen hushed their rowdy games while I was writing. I would have thrown myself into the Wye to save my children —even though I can't swim—yet I gave too little time to them.

For a few years—starting in Devon—I mixed a little painting with my poetry, just as relaxation. Visiting my mother in Carnkie I took her aback one day by saying I thought I would paint the mine stacks behind the house. "Why on earth should you want to do that, my sweetheart?" she exclaimed; then roared with laughter when I explained I didn't intend to plaster the stacks with paint. My hobby ended with a life class in Hereford. The first model was okay; I positioned myself shamelessly so I could look straight up between her legs; but the second model was ugly and had shaved her pubic mount. She looked like a plucked chicken. It was a choice between being turned off painting or being turned off women, and I opted for the first.

In '71, the year of *Logan Stone*, I flew with Peter Redgrove to the States for a short poetry tour. In Arizona, amid the desert cactuses, I met a girl whose long blonde hair was like an emanation of the harsh sunlight, blue sky, and stars as large as blossoms. The girl and the desert blended with the Red Indian poetry I encountered to form a purifying image.

> Like a kachina-mask
> you wear your beauty like a kachina-mask
> your beauty

the minute you are gone
desert rain
    red
    mariposa lilies
    astonished
    mariposa lilies
                (from *Sonoran Poems*)

But this was only five days outside the calendar. There was no room in my heart; the young woman who had told me, "You want too much, too soon," had begun to engrave herself into my life. Our relationship brought pain, both to herself and to Maureen, but it proved unremovable.

I wished she and my father could have met. I had a dream in which he appeared, not pale and ill as he had always looked in dreams before, but vibrantly alive.

My woman said to me
I feel so guilty
at never knowing your father

    why don't you let him
    come and fetch me on sunday
    for the big easter tea at your house
    instead of you?

        And have him come early
        then he can sleep with me
        if you don't mind

    Mind! I was very pleased and excited
    easter day parties at our house
    are terribly grim with the dead
    still in their grave clothes & still dying
    & just a cup of potato wine

When I met him from the cemetery
it was wonderful
to see him so much better & younger

so wiry and healthy &
filthy dirty from work & his carroty
hairtufts I'd forgotten
making his whole body glow like an indian brave

> but when it came to it
> I didn't like to ask him
> if he'd fetch my woman

> > because he'd forgotten the letter f
> > & fourteen years of death
> > makes driving strange & dangerous

> it might seem I was taking advantage
> I couldn't be open with him

and he
> humble as always reticent
> he didn't want to seem pushing

(Dream)

I was reticent with my children. The closer someone was to me, the more reticent I felt. I rejoiced at their successes, panicked over their sicknesses; but for some reason I found it easier to embrace a stranger. I'm sure they suffered because of my weird disability. Their mother suffered because of it too. My unfaithfulness might have been less painful had I been able to express my deep feeling for her.

Shlee godi. Floods swirled around us and we huddled close. We kept saying to local councillors anxious for our vote, "When are you going to do something about the flooding?" Eventually the river was dredged and the floodwater didn't reach us any more. We missed the closeness, the excitement, the Ark.

Every summer I took Denise on holiday to Cornwall. My mother didn't dare meet us at Carnkie, so I would fetch her to a drab motel for a lunch. My mistress's image became blended in my eyes with Cornwall: the stark splendour of Botallack with its ancient mine perched under the cliff, lapped by the Atlantic; the emerald sea of Porthcurno; the mysterious men-an-tol of the moors; the lush river valleys of the Fal, Helford and Fowey. But with her rather boyish face and dark, short, fringed hair, she also resembled Akhmatova, whose birthday she shared. By disliking the role, in her down-to-earth way, she became ever more deeply the Muse.

Like the delicately poised Logan Rock of Porthcurno, and like Cornwall itself threatening to break off from the mainland, our relationship was always imperilled yet seemed the stronger because of it.

> if it were one
> stone it would not be magical
> if it were two stones the attrition of
> rain cutting into its natural weakness too well
> it would not be magical if its massif could be set
> trembling neither two nor one for a moment only say
> the logging-point of night-fall it would be magical yet
> not miraculous small worlds may be born of such magic
> but that it can go on and on without ceasing dazzling
> the spectator with motionless motion neither two nor one
> neither one nor two doomed and unshakable on its point
> of infinity that is the miracle to be so weak
> a finger logs it what constant strength
> what force it takes to be a
> logan
> stone you and I what cold applied
> granite-fire logging on weakness no storm can move us
> (*Logan Stone*)

I had a study extension built on to the house. While the workmen were digging the foundations, their picks hit a skull. Two skeletons came to light, along with a shell and a boar's tusk. A pair of skeletal legs still rests under the coal cellar. The relics came from the medieval Franciscan Friary which gave its name to the avenue: Greyfriars. There are probably many more skeletons underlying the garden, including Owen Tudor, executed in Hereford and buried in the Greyfriars cemetery.

It was much more appealing and moving to learn that a poet, William Herbert, lived and presumably died (in 1333) where my house stands.

> Seththe He my robe tok,
> Also ich finde in Bok,
> He is to me ibounde:
> And helps he wole, ich wot,
> For Love the chartre wrot,
> And the enk orn of His wounde.

I framed and hung this verse from his *Orison to the Blessed Virgin*.

I needed all the divine help I could get. I found it hard enough to handle my divided life, but the women who divided it found it harder. My children were suffering too. I hated causing pain; it was a long time since I had torn the wings off flies.

There is a dreamlike quality about events following my mother's death in '75. Vaguely I recall divorcing Maureen, marrying Denise and then divorcing her; yet since nothing changed materially—I continued to live with Maureen, continued to live apart from Denise—the changes could, for all I know, have been an actual dream. One thing is clear, that Ross, my second son, was born during this disturbed and dreamlike period.

It isn't surprising that my house seemed to become haunted. Caitlin, in her late teens, heard me come into the house at around ten in the evening, dump a briefcase in the kitchen, then climb upstairs. She wondered why I hadn't put my head around the lounge door to say hello. But I was still at Denise's house.

Maureen kept a row of porcelain cups and saucers on a lounge shelf. One night from our beds we heard a crashing downstairs; we rushed to look. Two of the cups had lifted clean off their saucers and come to rest, several feet away, uptilted each side of the front television legs, equidistant from them. Nothing could have caused their flight; plodding old Thomas, who never leapt around anything, was slumbering in the hall where we had left her.

I drifted, with a sense of unreality, of fiction. The pattern of my life seemed to have evolved outside of my will and intention. I couldn't connect the fifty-year-old man with the five-year-old child. The unreality, the mystery of events, struck me forcefully on a Cornish holiday when Ross was four. We visited a National Trust garden at Glendurgan. There was a maze, and our son disappeared into it. Then we strolled down through the magnificent trees and shrubs to a pebbly beach. Not until then did I connect Glendurgan with Durgan, and remembered a flash of pebbles.

> The Handkerchief or Ghost Tree
> stands among Monterey pines,
> the Californian redwood, the Chilean
> Fire Bush, the Whitebeam, the Maidenhair
> Tree, in the Garden of Glendurgan
> that slopes to the Helford River,
> to the quiet beach of Durgan.
>
> I should remember Durgan.
> I was taken here as a child,
> many times, and the word 'Durgan'
> brought joy to my parents' eyes;
> but coming here today, carrying
> a child in my arms, I can recognise
> nothing of this enchanted
> estuary. I can remember only
> a flash of pebbles, and being carried
> in someone's arms.
>
> When my father died,
> and I returned to the hospital
> to collect his clothes,
> I found in the breast pocket
> of his laundered pyjamas
> a screwed-up handkerchief
> still wringing with the sweat
> I had watched pour out of him.

Before he started dying
mysteriously he said:
'My way is clear.'
My sensible Protestant mother
saw a nun, framed
in the bedroom door, warning her
she would always be sleeping alone.

The small child runs
into the garden maze, and vanishes.
We hear his voice, and glimpse
now and again his merry face
through gaps in the laurel.
These lives . . . these lives that come
and go mysteriously, as the laurel leaves
shine and gloom in the cloudy
sunlight through the tall trees,

this convocation of
the world's trees, massing now
into one, without losing their distinct
character, in the walk down to Durgan.
(*The Handkerchief or Ghost Tree*)

My life was made of divisions; I was twinned, like the
offspring of the mysterious Italian painter. One division,
which I had liked—that of teacher and writer—had been
destroyed against my will. I lived in a place that still seemed
alien, after twenty years, yet I couldn't quite make up my
mind to move back to Cornwall, which I loved. I thought I
would test the water with one toe, by looking for a holiday
home.

There was another division, between prose and poetry,
where I was hopelessly muddled. Prose seemed to be winning,
and I wasn't sure I liked it.

As for the most deep-rooted division of all, there seemed no
possible solution. Maureen was important to me; she connected me to my youth; we could reach each other's minds,
conjure the same memories. Our Cornishness was a bond; we

laughed at the same jokes, shared a sense of the ridiculous; responded to the same nostalgic music. Her faith in and respect for my work made it possible for me to write. If it was not love I felt for her, the word had no meaning. I had a strong commitment to my family. But Denise and Ross were also my family.

"In Samoa," I remind my analyst, "they have a three-day Yam Festival in which anything goes. Strict monogamy rules for the rest of the year, but during the Yam Festival anybody can fuck anybody. I think that's an excellent arrangement; it satisfies the human need for commitment but also for freedom and exploration . . . I *think* it's Samoa . . . Erica Jong told me about it. We joked about the guy who has the bad luck to have flu during the Yam Festival; he'd think, Christ, I've got to wait another year . . .

"I believe marriage should be permanent; but then there should be no sanction against taking lovers. I even quite like the idea of arranged marriages; because then you're almost bound to look for passion elsewhere. Passion is vital, and I don't see how it can be reconciled with the familiarity of marriage: the wife washing her husband's socks, the husband seeing his wife in curlers. Shaw said that marriage combines the maximum of temptation with the maximum of opportunity. That's stupid; it doesn't make sense. It shows how crass he was."

"There *are* marriages," she says, "which are based on a mutual erotic excitement, a sexual obsession."

"Really? Well, I haven't come across any. I do believe, in theory, in the *hieros gamos*, the sacred marriage; it's just that they rarely happen. I loathe the idea of exclusivity in a relationship, the idea that you possess someone and they possess you. I'm capable of jealousy, I can become insanely jealous if I think my position is threatened, but I wouldn't let it get in the way of a woman's right to have an affair."

"What does sex mean to you?" she asks.

I rub my thigh, considering the question. "Certainly far more than the physical act. That's relatively unimportant.

Holding hands with someone, or just looking into their eyes, can be sexual. I prefer the word erotic. It's where we are most vulnerable and sensitive, most open to wonder and to the sacred. Where the microcosm opens itself to the cosmic."

I move my left hand from my thigh to clasp my other hand over my chest. "Of course, AIDS has ruined sex for a generation. But it isn't sex which is the villain; sex doesn't cause the disease. The villain is a virus. Just as God can use sex, in coupling with Leda or Mary, to advance creation and goodness, so a virus will use it to spread destruction and evil. Both seek out our weak point; but since ultimately I believe God is stronger than viruses, I must think sex is good. And it *can* be as good with a stranger as with someone you love. Though of course, when there is love as well, then you can occasionally reach a mountain peak . . ."

She remains silent. I find myself wondering if she ever reaches a mountain peak with her husband.

"But perhaps AIDS will be an *aid* to eroticism. People won't be able to leap into bed quite so readily, so they'll pay more attention to the rituals of sex. Rituals are important. Sex is theatre. We've lost sight of it in the zipless fuck. Victor Hugo was wise when he used an erotic metaphor for the curtain going up in a theatre: *Je voyais enlever la jupe de mon âme.*"

It must surely be time to go. I'm aware of talking on desperately, fearful of our silences. What more can I say about my attitude to sex?

"Lust, Madam; sheer lust."

"It's time."

"Yes."

There are limits to the amount of guilt a person can bear. Confused with my guilt over my divided life was a self-deceiving belief that the women who divided it *ought* to find their lives tolerable. Maureen, I felt, had a decent home and standard of living; she could afford an occasional foreign holiday with her friends. Oh, I could see she was probably lonely, some of the time, and might prefer to go on holiday with *me*; weekend breaks *en famille* to Venice and Istanbul hardly measured up to a Mediterranean cruise. Yet no marriage—and ours still seemed essentially a marriage—was perfect. Surely she knew I valued her good cooking, her home-making, our comradeship, her unswerving loyalty? And I believed I too was loyal, in my way. I knew she had passions I hadn't been able to touch, at least since our earliest days; but nothing stood in the way of her expressing those passions with others.

As for Denise, she had a fulfilling career, and a child. I knew she resented the way I could pick up my book and leave at the end of an evening; yet she saw as much of me as many a wife, say of a long-distance lorry driver; had good holidays; and she didn't have to feed me or wash my socks.

I under-estimated the need both had to unify their lives. I tried to blind myself to their craving for normality: the one's desire for the security of a wedding ring, the other's pleasure in the domesticity of a well-kept garden.

Also confused with my guilt and my self-exoneration was admiration for them both. I admired their tenacity, their stubborn survival, their unsullied pride.

I couldn't see any end to the situation. And somewhere, in the midst of it all, I had the energy to write. From the grit came a kind of pearl. And that grit only verged on the intolerable at Christmas, when I needed to be in two places at once. I'd feel a desolation as I drove along deserted streets, sometimes making fresh tyre-marks in a thin mantle of snow.

Inconceivable that I would still be doing this at sixty, seventy. Yet it seemed vital, not for my sake alone, that neither relationship 'win', neither of them 'lose'.

Maureen was the rock, which must not crumble.

Denise and I often quarrelled and sometimes parted, but we soon drew together again. I couldn't stay away for long; whoever I happened to be with, briefly, always I saw her face, heard her voice. Sex, whether bitter from estrangement, sweet from reconciliation, or buried in memory and imagination, was only a symbol of something inexpressibly binding . . .

Let me ache, indicate, simper who touched
your warm cunt, whisper, let on now,
disperse them into our love.
Who did you? it's all the same:
deep pricks or, islands of assiduous fictions,
disperse them into our love.

Am I in her, pummel her, he fucked you, ah
total and thousands of indecent, poked it in
did he, turgid and slewed, my girl, you right
there immixed with another, convoke it actually
wrapt round him, feel his engorgement
displacing your space, cleaving your achable
cleft better than this, novel then sweetly
a habit, why that's my spirit,
my fluttering clairvoyant, my fat ghost.

(Flesh)

NINETEEN

Callers

"I saw this fantastic clairvoyant last night!" says Joan, my housekeeper. We're having a coffee and a chat in my kitchen. "She's only a simple woman, living in a council-house, but she's marvellous, Don!"

Midwinter sunlight, striking through the window, sparkles on her gypsyish earrings and bangles. An attractive, red-haired divorcée, she brightens my house with flowers or berries, but also with her own smart, exotic appearance. Her elegant high-heeled shoes may not be particularly practical for cleaning and scrubbing, but they're good for my morale; I look forward to her appearance, in both senses, three afternoons a week. She irons my shirts to a blare of Tchaikovsky or Wagner. When I'm alone here, somehow I don't have the impulsion to break the silence with music.

She chatters on about the clairvoyant's stunning performance; I smile and nod, without taking it all in. When she drifts to a halt I say, "Could you fix up an appointment for me? But don't tell her anything about me, not even my name. And I'd rather it weren't here."

She goes to the phone in the hall, dials, and I hear her say that a gentleman would like to consult her. The meeting is arranged at Joan's house.

I feel in need of clairvoyance. Maureen's autumnal departure was strange. Usually, when a person leaves home to live with someone else, there's a period of adjustment, a half-way house, in which divorces are arranged, and so on. It was different with us. Our life appeared normal to the end. I was going to spend a few days in Cornwall, where I'd bought a holiday cottage at St Erth, a village near St Ives. Maureen made my breakfast toast as usual; tearful, we pecked a kiss;

as I went to the car I tried to ignore the packing case and the coffee morning friends arriving to help. While we were driving back from Cornwall, on All Souls' Day, I knew she was getting married, with Sean and Caitlin as fairly reluctant witnesses, having her reception, and leaving for the honeymoon.

It was a very strange feeling. But we remain friends. The children and I even shared a Boxing Day dinner with her and her new husband, and it was amicable. She is happy and deserves happiness.

For me the winter has been weird and silent and sad; I've hated the long hours of darkness. But I've survived. Denise, though a frantically busy teacher and mother, has cooked for me most evenings; we're planning in the spring to look for a permanent house in Cornwall. The winter is at its deepest and coldest, but at least the evenings are drawing out. Surely the worst is over.

When I'm not pacing around empty rooms, I huddle in my study; but I no longer like the room, it no longer feels like a haven. I'm forcing myself to write the last book of my Quartet, a satirical farce based on the recent superpower summit in Geneva. 'Writing', though, doesn't seem the right word: I'm typing it with a kind of dementia. It's crude, over-the-top stuff, akin to my feelings; I can't stop for thought, for revision; the subtleties of a novel are now beyond me.

My laboriously evolved novels about *improvisatori* have reached an unexpected climax. I'm like a frenzied *improvisatore* on a stage, gabbling into the darkness.

The sharp-featured clairvoyant drinks wine, smokes, and gives me her initial patter, her eyes glancing around as if waiting for a spirit. She is as homely and simple as Doris Stokes, as all mediums. I'm satisfied she doesn't know me from Adam; I am just a friend of Joan, who sits poised with a pad and pen ready to take notes.

My first otherworld caller arrives: Viv, the medium, is

glancing past my right shoulder. "I'm getting a John. Do you know anyone called John?"

Everyone knows a John. John the Baptist? Uncle John, my mother's brother-in-law? But I can't imagine him standing there in his gaiters and dirty collarless white shirt.

"I'm a good speller," Uncle John would boast.

"Spell prominent."

"SDQURJCWVT."

"That's right!"

He would beam. "I'm a good speller!"

No, I don't think Uncle John would drop in.

"Then you know a Chris. You must know a Chris."

Only an attractive doctor's wife in Cheshire, an ex-student, still very much alive as far as I know.

"Well, never mind, these are often distant relatives from the past. They just popped in to say hello . . . I'm seeing someone more clearly. I'd say he was a very neatly dressed gentleman; always neatly dressed. He looks a bit like you."

My father? He dressed neatly at the weekends. When we came back from Australia, Mother made him change from a cloth cap to a trilby.

"Yes, I think it's your father. And beside him, not quite so clear, I would say this is your mother. A big woman . . ."

She was quite small, but plump: I suppose that might count as big in the spirit world.

"Her hair is grey."

"Yes." Actually it was white, but I don't want to discourage her too much.

"Would they be from Yorkshire? I think I'm getting a Yorkshire accent."

"No, they were Cornish."

"Ah! I *thought* it was a strong accent . . . Your father isn't an elderly man. I'd say he was quite young when he passed over. Late fifties or sixty?"

"Fifty-nine."

"Your mother was older; she looks about seventy, early seventies."

"Seventy-two." Now *this* is more like it.

"And she didn't have a long illness; I mean she didn't suffer for a long time. She had a good strong heart."

My nape prickles.

"Your Mum isn't saying much; it's your Dad who's doing most of the talking. Oh, he's a nice gentleman! He thought a lot of you! He says you've been through a bad time—or are about to go through a bad time, but it'll come out all right."

I nod. I *have* had a bad time.

"He's saying something about November. You had some bereavement, or sorrow, that's connected with the month of November. Can you think? It could have been any year."

Racking my brains, I can't think of any sorrowful, bereaved November. Father and mother, both January; Andrew, June; Auntie Cecie, December.

"No, I don't think so."

She tells me to think about it later. It may come.

I shall have to have an operation; or—perhaps she sees my alarmed face—see a doctor, about my stomach. But I mustn't worry, it will turn out all right.

"You have plans to move," she says. "Does it involve two, or even three, houses?"

"Yes."

If we buy a house in Cornwall, I shall have to sell my house here and the holiday cottage. It's been weighing on me. How extraordinary for her to pick that up!

"He thinks your plans are good. But you shouldn't sell your house too soon." Her eyes twinkle as she adds, "He's saying to me, Of course he *will*!"

I'm going to be surrounded by men in dark suits, professional people, maybe lawyers. I won't like it—is it something to do with a will? But I'll get through it.

Unlikely. I don't even have a solicitor, and I fear making a will.

She sees or hears about six brothers. And here is a young man who says he's very close to me in some way. "He died young."

"That would be one of my uncles—he was killed in a plane crash, and when I came along I was given his name."

"Yes, well, he's a very lively young man, very cheerful and bubbling over. He just popped in to say hello, he's gone again now. I have London coming up—does the name Janet, living in London, mean anything to you?"

"No."

"There's *something* to do with London . . . Do you know someone there? Do your children live there? Ah, I thought so! You've got two children, haven't you? Is your daughter a nurse? Well, chiropody is close: I knew she was in the medical profession, your mother was telling me. She knew your daughter, didn't she? She's a very sensible girl, your Mum says, and she's going to be all right. She will be travelling overseas. But your Mum's a bit worried about your son. He's in some bad company. Is he in one of the professions?"

"He's a professional lay-about!" I joke, rather unfairly, since he is writing his first novel. "He's just left University."

"So he's in the professional area." She nods. Nothing is ever *wrong*; meaningless names, of which several float in, can always belong to distant long-dead relatives. I observe her mind working a little like a poet's, or as I imagine an analyst's must work. "She's a bit worried about him, but he's going to pull out of it okay, probably by travelling a lot."

Many of her statements are uncannily shrewd. I know my mother would approve of Caitlin's good sense, and worry about Sean's bohemian friends. She used to worry if I had two or three sherries. Can they really have survived death? Do they stand at my shoulder?

She tells me I've been looking at old photographs. It's true I opened a drawer today and caught sight of the brown album which goes back to their Californian idyll. The medium nods. "They just mentioned it to show you they're with you, they're watching over you."

They're nice people, she says, and friendly; but they're not coming through to her as openly as people sometimes do. Perhaps they were rather reserved?

I deny it.

She's almost at the end of the hour. She wishes she could get my father's name. It came up once, but it's slipped out of her mind. She purses her brow. "Is it Fred?"

I grin, shaking my head. She meditates again.

"I'm getting very strongly the name Harold."

"Good God!"

"Oh, and your mother is saying to me her hair wasn't grey but white."

"Yes!"

She crooks her hands rheumatically. "And she's saying, of course you know at the end I couldn't do much because of these old hands."

As I drive home through dark, slushy streets, I hear my mother saying "these old hands". I almost *saw* the hands, and her wrinkled face. That extraordinary final *bravura* display! I'd agreed my mother's hair was grey: what made her change it? And Harold!

I can even imagine my father saying 'Fred' jokingly, and laughing, before giving his real name.

My house is lit up. I always leave lights on when going out in the evenings, to make it look welcoming. It never welcomes me, though; it is estranged from itself. It takes a woman to warm a house with her spirit.

November! Good grief! That was when she left!

How absurd and strange that I didn't think of it!

Thomas, the old cat, is waiting to be let in. She is just bright enough to go out by the flap, but not in. She mews soundlessly. I stoop to stroke her. She is thin, and her turned-up eyes, yellowed in the darkness, look orphaned.

TWENTY

Blanks

He said goodbye to his uncle and left the institute. Outside, the evening was clear and still summery bright, with only a softening of dusk. The village seemed empty, suspended in silence; a faint sound of hymn-singing came from the Sunday school, where the religious and elderly had gathered, and those too poor to own television sets. Behind the village, the grouped and stately mine stacks prepared themselves for the solemnity of nightfall.

He looked quickly up at the institute clock and saw it was a quarter past eight. A rough calculation told him he ought to arrive only about ten minutes after the time he had promised. Bridget wouldn't mind that, particularly if he greeted her in a nice way, with a 'light' in his eyes. He thought tenderly how much she loved him, worshipped him indeed, and shook off the cramping knowledge of the mutual love and worship they were soon publicly to avow. The formality of it grated, all but destroyed. He loved her, in his way, deep down; but he didn't want to settle down yet; he valued his freedom too highly. These wedding arrangements were destructive, too. No matter how considerate he tried to be, he was bound to hurt somebody's feelings. However far he extended the circle of invited guests, there was still the outer fringe of people who *ought* to have been invited, and who would take their omission as a personal slur. It was very depressing.

Then it struck him as slightly ridiculous that he should be getting married at all, and life didn't seem so bad: it was at least amusing, and there were compensations.

A young and attractive woman was walking up the road towards him. He had never seen her before, and this was a matter of some surprise, because young and attractive women did not often take it into their head to stroll through the village alone. There was nothing to attract people, except on Boxing Day, when the local Hunt assembled nearby, and it was quite an occasion. But this was midsummer.

It was even more surprising that she smiled, and was obviously preparing to speak to him.

"Could you tell me, please," she said in pleasant, diffident Cornish tones, "where Mrs Pryor lives? I'm told it's just above the Sunday school." She gestured faintly towards the hymn-singing.

He didn't know, but he wanted to help her very much. He told her to wait a moment, while he went back inside the institute to ask.

"Do you know where a Mrs Pryor lives?" he asked his uncle. "There's a lady outside who wants to know."

His uncle reached for his trilby, so he cut in sharply with: "Do you know where she lives?" The flat question took his uncle aback, as he had intended it to, and he dropped his trilby. "Well no," he said, "not exactly; but I think it's up past Primitive: two houses with their backs to the road. I think Mrs Pryor lives there."

"That's okay then. She can come with me, I'll show her where it is."

He went out, pleased at having kept her to himself.

"We're not sure where it is," he told her, "but we think it's up past the chapel. I'm going that way, so you can come with me."

"That's kind of you. I'm putting you to a lot of trouble."

"No, no trouble at all. I've got to go that way."

They walked shyly together, but it was surprising how quickly they got used to the situation. She felt flattered by his politeness. He talked a little self-consciously, but with a beautiful accent—not at all like a native of these parts. Yet there was no 'side', no attempt to appear uppish. His bearing was distinguished yet natural; he must be home from college, she thought. Living in the coombe beneath the village, she rarely met any men, except her husband. It was a very cut-off place. The polite young man was such a change. They might almost be sweethearts out for a walk.

"It's quite a long way," she said. "They told me it was just above the Sunday school."

"Yes, but there are two Sunday schools, Wesley and Primitive. You can see the Primitive up there."

The road bent away from the village and mounted the hill. There was a farmhouse on the left, and facing you the white front of the chapel gleamed from behind a few scant trees. It was a strangely affecting part of the road. Life always seemed to take on a fuller significance when he came to it, especially on his way back from Bridget's in the late evening. Perhaps it was because it was the last lonely stretch before home, and his senses quickened at the thought of the tasty supper and flask of tea that would be waiting for him. Then there was a tree which stood out in bleak dignity against the faint glow of street lights from the distant town: and the mine stacks too, rising dimly. Two or three times he had been frightened, but also deeply stirred, by the bulk of two draught horses looming up un-expectedly on the mound above him as he turned the corner. If they should fall or leap down they might easily kill someone; but they just stood there motionless and far-seeing, staring hour after hour into gulfs of darkness. He would look back at them, envying their self-possession. Another time he saw two cats crouched in a ditch, one on top of the other. The top one darted away as he approached, and stood watching him from the hedge. The other lay still, and he saw it was dead, though there were no marks on it. Another memory haunted him from this part of the road. There had been an old man who was slightly mad, but not mad enough, they said, to be put away. He carried a gnarled stick and wheeled a bicycle with a flat tyre, and his eyes were quite crazy. One night, to his horror, he saw the unmistakable shape of bicycle and stick and old man coming up the road towards him in the dark. He could do nothing, only pass him silently and hope for the best. But just as he got past there was a crazy, murderous snarl in his ear, and another, and he ran and ran, all the way down into the village, and did not stop till he came to his own gate, his heart bursting. He could still hear the old man snarling in the distance, and all the dogs began to bark, and the old man started barking too. The next week he hit the bonnet of a police car with his stick, and was put away.

Naturally such memories did not occupy his mind at this moment, but the strangely charged atmosphere of the place added perhaps to his interest and excitement. On this road, he felt, anything could happen.

"I hope you're not scared of dogs?" he remarked. "A couple up here'll bark your head off."

"Oh dear, I'm scared of my life of them. I don't know what I shall do on the way back—I think if we don't find the right house I'll go on with you."

He glanced swiftly down at her; but her blue eyes looked guilelessly into his. He wanted to say, "It would be a pleasure," or something like that, but at the moment he was tongue-tied, and mumbled something in his throat. He hoped the dogs would bark their fiercest, to see what she would do, and what he would do; but as luck would have it, they made not a sound.

"You come from Pendear?" he asked, mentioning the nearest town.

"No, I live in the Coombe. You know where Mrs Levett used to live?"

"Yes."

"Well, we've got her house now. It's off the road."

The way she said this last inconsequential phrase told him that she was lonely. It was more, now, than showing a lady to a house; he felt close to her, protective and comforting.

"Do you smoke?" she asked.

"No," he replied, then laughed shortly: "You want a cigarette?"

"No, I've got some in my handbag, but I'm too lazy to light up. Redvers wanted to know what I wanted cigarettes for to go up and see Mrs Pryor, but I took them all the same."

He vaguely wondered who Redvers was. He tried to look at her hands, but could only see the left. That seemed to be ringless. But he wasn't sure which hand wore the wedding ring.

They went past moist-smelling hayfields, and reached the two houses with their backs to the road where his uncle thought a Mrs Pryor might live. There was one tiny window high up on the uneven, white-washed surface, and an odd-looking chimney breathed out smoke. A gate and path led round to the back, or rather the front, of the house. There was a low sound of voices, but he couldn't tell whether any of them belonged to Mrs Pryor or not. He hoped that they didn't. From what she had said—"If we don't find the right house I think I'll go on with you"—he thought that she might hope so as well. The faintest gesture of indecision came from her.

"Could you wait here," she said, "while I go in and find out."

He waited, and heard her voice mingle with the others. He knew it was the right house. She reappeared round the side and again he noticed the clear, bright gaze of her blue eyes. "This is the house all right," she said. For a moment they hung there, silence between them; then she smiled and thanked him conventionally, and went in.

The next morning he was shaving, with the bathroom door open, and his mother was ironing.

"Who lives in Mrs Levett's house now?" he asked casually.

"I don't know," his mother replied, "why?"

"A woman was up here last night asking for Mrs Pryor, and she said she lived in Mrs Levett's house."

"I don't know. I think they're strangers."

In the afternoon he purposely made a detour through the Coombe on his way to Pendear, where he had to arrange taxis for the guests. He examined the house carefully as he passed, but saw nobody, only a line of washing swinging gently in the garden. He smiled ironically—'better luck next time'. Or if not next time, the time after. Next month, or next year, *someone* would inevitably respond. All at once he felt a motion of panic, and strove to control his breathing. He saw before him a lifetime of petty lies and deceit, and possible tragedy to others; and all without the slightest ill-will, with a perfectly good 'heart'. A lifetime of petty infidelity, consummated usually in imagination. If only he could feel responsible, if only he had principles. Perhaps the marriage service would help. Suddenly not even the deeply known and loved countryside through which he passed could prevent him from feeling very frightened and very much alone.

I came across the copy of *Isis*—November 1958—while rummaging in a battered and cobwebbed suitcase from the attic. It contained my first published work, my only short story. My mind flew back; no one had told me the story had been accepted; I'd bought the magazine at Oxford station, browsed through it, and been thrilled to find *The Opportunist* by Donald Thomas.

Reading it again after almost thirty years was a strange experience. I'd completely forgotten the adventure or non-adventure it related, but it flooded back; I grieved that I'd been so shy; why hadn't I said, "Couldn't you give Mrs Pryor a miss?"? But that would have meant letting Maureen down; I was faithful and faithless.

Of course the ending was terribly pompous. Far from 'worshipping' me, I feel sure Maureen had her own doubts. She had other, rather livelier admirers; she too must have been influenced by her elders telling her I was a nice young man.

What moved me most about the story was to recognise —despite the Lawrentian echoes—my voice. That didn't happen with most of the execrable early poems I found in the other magazines that tumbled out of the old suitcase. But the prose style—that was me, essentially no different from the man I am now. That surprised me.

In this later solitude and anxiety I wondered if I ought to have found an uncharacteristic courage and broken off the engagement. But whenever Caitlin or Sean came home for a visit I ceased to wonder; the marriage had been fruitful, it held a meaning. It was part of the given life, like the Australian tree of my adolescence.

Sean's visits were always shortlived and impromptu.

He came without warning, usually for a reunion with his Hereford friends, and left without ceremony. Dressed out-landishly, ear-ringed, crop-haired, he neither asked if it was convenient to come nor if I'd like him to stay longer; yet, camping in his tiny bedroom as if he'd never been away, he made the ghost-house inhabited for a few hours.

On one visit he rather shyly gave me a typescript of his novel to read. I started it apprehensively, fearing I'd have to pretend enjoyment, but I soon relaxed; I found a dazzlingly poetic style which, though it showed the influence of Joyce, was already his own. I knew it couldn't be easy to follow in his father's footsteps and still have it all to do. I admired his dedication and envied his devil-may-care independence.

"I've been dreaming."

"Tell me."

"I was in a large, rambling house with Denise and her parents. They were planning to go out, but I was to stay in and feed a baby. An ex-student called in—no one I recognised; pale, rather austere. She offered to come back later and help me with the baby. It was an obvious sexual advance, and I wasn't sure whether it would be worth the trouble and danger. But when Denise's father said he was going to stay in too, I was annoyed. However, his memory isn't what it was; I thought, even if I went to bed with the girl right in front of him, he'd have forgotten it by the time the others got back.

"But actually she leapt into bed with me right there and then! Cuddling up to me. I had to grimace, as if to say, It's just her fun, it wasn't my idea. Fortunately they took it in good spirits. Denise and her mother went out; the ex-student left, promising to be back. I warmed milk for the baby's bottle, and tasted it; it was mawkish and unpleasant. There was a knock on the door, and in came the ex-student, followed by a trail of other young people in harlequin outfits. She'd just been teasing me. They danced laughing around me as I stood in my pinny, ready for the feed.

"Later I was driving with Denise's mother. She opened the

glove-compartment and exposed to view some dirty babies' bottles. I was embarrassed that my secret was out. And then, the people in harlequin were showing me what looked like a turd made of milk. They said if I swallowed it it would help to prevent cancer of the bowel. That's it."

I stare up at a grey sky through the angled window-panes. Silence. I add, "The baby never made an appearance."

"It didn't have to," she murmurs.

"How do you mean?"

"It was you who tasted the milk."

"Ah! You mean . . . ?"

"Uh-huh."

"Who was the student?"

"It seems to me very much a dream about psychoanalysis."

"I see! Yes, she could have been a younger version of you. And the house could have been this one."

"She is helping you with the baby," she offers as confirmation.

"But then why does she let me down, by turning up with clownishly dressed people?"

"This is your ambivalence. You're still not sure you can trust me."

"And what about my secret hoard of babies' bottles?"

"Well, where do you keep such magazines as the one you brought back from Munich?"

"Not in the glove-compartment of my car."

"In a sock-drawer, perhaps? There are many forms of love-substitutes . . . It's a hopeful dream; at the end you're being shown a way through your constipation, your block."

"You mean by eating milky shit."

"It's time."

With Denise, Ross, and a Welsh couple who often share our holidays, I'm flying by private helicopter to St Michael's Mount in Cornwall. But we land on a West Indian island. Visiting a poor village school, I find to my amazement and joy that they know of my father. He lived on the island for some

years, half-a-century ago. He came from California with a
paralysed woman, whom he nursed tenderly. He painted. The
school has kept some of his paintings, on cheap exercise-book
paper. The teacher who is talking to us produces three of the
paintings. One is a Cornish landscape, another an abstract, the
third a nude. They show a rich talent; I'm thrilled when the
teacher makes me a gift of one of them. He says we might find
others around the island: for instance, at the garage just down
the road.

We go out into the brilliant heat. Down the palm-treed road
is the rough shack of a garage; we head for it. I stroll with
Roger, our Welsh friend. As is his way he thinks carefully
before making a judgement. At last, breaking our silence, he
says, "Those paintings—impressive."

"Yes, aren't they? And what I find most moving is that *they*
thought he was in California all those years, when actually he
was here. Which means that, although we think he's dead, that
he's nowhere—it isn't so!"

"Then," I say to my analyst, "it got mixed up with a James
Bond-type situation. Lots of shooting. And again there's a
woman involved. I don't know who the paralysed woman
was. But it's clear what the dream means in general. I've been
told he had artistic talent, and wanted to go to the Art School
in Redruth; but they were too poor, he had to find work."

I sigh; my stomach gurgles. "And another dream, last
night. It was war. We had some Nazi soldiers and some
collaborators lined up. The collaborators were hanged without mercy, but the Nazis somehow escaped. They were
concentrated in the dining room at 'St Martin's'. I crept
around from our part of the house, cradling a machine-gun,
stooping past the windows so I shouldn't be seen. The Nazis
came at me and I opened fire; but I had no effect. Either the
bullets jammed or they were blanks. I kept firing but the Nazis
kept on coming, streaming past."

She reflects on the dream, then says, "There's a lot of anger,
a lot of secret rage. War is a legitimate excuse for killing
people. It occurs to me that you bring collaborators into it
because some of them could be female . . ."

"No, they were all men; it was an all-male dream."

"I'd say your mother was frightened of your penis. She made you cover it up. I also remember you talking about *The Water Babies*—the little dirty sweep emerging into a bedroom where there was a pure, clean maiden in bed. Your mother was frightened of blood and shit and mess; she measured out the milk, never let you get in touch with her body. You saw her corseted; I'd guess you thought she had a penis hidden under it; you saw women as some kind of powerful, almost hermaphrodite creatures . . ."

"But I did see her when she was on the toilet, once. I saw she didn't have a—wee-wee, as she called it."

"And what did you think had happened to it?"

"Well, I know what Freud would say. That it had been cut off. But I just thought—she doesn't have a wee-wee."

Somewhere beyond the window a jet, presumably from the nearby RAF station, screams across the sky.

"Of course I found the war terribly exciting. That plane brought it back. Last night I was watching *Fortunes of War* on TV; and when the ack-ack guns started I felt that tremor of excitement just as I used to. And I suppose the overall tension may have hidden tensions within our house. I don't know, I don't know . . . So you think my gun wouldn't fire because my mother was afraid of my penis?"

"Yes."

"Nature gave to women so much power that the law did not dare to add to it. Dr Johnson."

She chuckles. "It's time."

TWENTY-ONE

Stone Guests

Soon after my encounter with the clairvoyant I fell ill, as she had predicted. Poised to adapt Pushkin's *The Stone Guest* as a libretto, I found I had two stone guests of my own: one blocking my right kidney, the other almost filling my left. I went to London and saw two men in dark suits; I was to see many men in dark suits over the next year.

My consultants—who happened to be called John and Chris—were anxious. The stones could be dissolved, partly by hoicking out, partly with use of a new stone-crumbling machine, the lithotripter; but it would be difficult; I was more ill than I realised. They admired my stoicism.

I confessed I didn't feel at all stoical. I was terrified I would die if operated on. I explained how my father had had a cerebral haemorrhage after a 'routine' prostatectomy; and my Uncle Leslie, ten years later, had taken fright when he knew he would have to have the same operation. He had tried to avoid my father's fate by going into a private hospital—and died in exactly the same way.

I strongly resembled them both.

Returning to my hotel at Paddington after the consultation, I rang Caitlin and agitatedly begged her to come. Next morning I was to have a nephrostomy, a tube inserted in the right kidney to drain pus. The only consolation was that it could be done by local anaesthetic: I was terrified of being 'put under'. My daughter arrived and tried to calm me.

I felt the prodding of the thick needle and winced. "Sorry, old chap, you'll have to have a general." I was wheeled and elevated back to my private room, and had several hours in which to contemplate extinction. After the pre-med, I must have appeared corpse-like when they wheeled me down again, for, in the lift, I heard one of the nurses say absentmindedly, "The basement", then chuckle at her error. "Oh, no!" I saw a grisly humour in it. But I would be down there soon.

When I came round slowly in my room I was in great pain and shaking in an uncontrollable *rigor*. Caitlin's face appeared vaguely, also a nurse's and a doctor's. I was attempting to say, "Pain, pain". The doctor said, "We'll give you an injection in a minute." The *rigor* went on and on.

When I awoke again it was night and I had a marvellous calm, floaty feeling. I wanted a drink, which they wouldn't give me, but otherwise I felt terribly peaceful. I didn't know why a young male nurse kept dropping in, looking concerned. I had septicaemia and a high fever.

Blood dripped into a bag. They hoped it would turn to urine. I couldn't stand up; but after a night at Caitlin's flat I could manage to struggle to Hereford in the train. Denise met me, and stayed at my house to nurse me. In the bag at my thigh, red turned to amber.

I returned to London for stone-hoicking and crumbling at the Lithotripter Clinic. Another day of terror, but I survived the anaesthetic, waking momentarily to see a minute crystal between a nurse's thumb and fingers. Next morning I ate a hearty breakfast and rang home. Denise's happiness, describing her anxious calls through the three-hour operation, warmed me. I felt wonderfully good about her. We had a weekend break at a hotel, in which I couldn't walk far and dripped urine everywhere, but felt as much in love as I had done twenty years before.

The expert surgeons started in on the left kidney's giant staghorn. After the first operation I came round to another long, uncontrollable *rigor*. Sean, sitting at the foot of the bed, alternately begged an awkward coloured nurse to do something and buried his face in the *Guardian*. I understood and was amused. In the morning, cajoled into staggering to the bathroom, I collapsed. Still, there was only one operation to go; the mysterious and magical lithotripter would pulverise the rest of the staghorn with underwater lasers.

My chest, when I awoke, wouldn't breathe properly;

my heart fluttered weakly. "I'm going to die! I'm going to die!"

"No you're not."

A buxom, attractive staff nurse seized me to haul me from trolley to bed. My half-paralysed body rolled with her yielding flesh. "Oh, Mr Thomas!" she exclaimed as I held on tight to her, helplessly, feeling a faint but amazing lust for her soft body.

A second nurse crouched, adjusting tubes and bags. The staff nurse, climbing off the bed, stooped to help her; then jumped away, saying to her in humorous rebuke, "You're looking up my skirt!" She moved to the foot of the bed and repeated for my benefit, smiling, "She was looking up my skirt!"

With a gargantuan effort I got my mouth to half-articulate: "Lucky." The nurses grinned.

I thought of my father. "Nice . . ." It was all too eerie. I struggled to expand my lungs and quell my heart-murmur; I heard blood hissing in my neck. "Can't breathe . . ."

"You should try to go to sleep. You'll feel better when you wake up."

Mustn't sleep. "I shall die if I go to sleep."

The buxom staff nurse bent over me sympathetically. "You've been through a lot."

Sheba's Breasts. It was as if one of her breasts held life, the other death. I didn't know which I was going to suck. She gave me a sedative, and I fell asleep.

One doctor said it would be a few days before I felt well; a second said a few weeks; a third, three months. I suppose I was an unusual case.

For weeks I spent most of each day in bed. I couldn't get my walking legs back, and generally felt rougher than I ought to feel. I was convinced something was wrong. Tinnitus hissed in my ears. My Hereford GP diagnosed depression and anxiety and prescribed a drug. It didn't help; nor, at first, did a holiday in Cornwall with Denise, Ross, and some friends. I paced around constantly—my legs were strong at last—in a delirium of agitation. One afternoon, being driven to Porthleven, I was convinced I was going mad; my head was jangled and bursting. When I thought I must scream, the blue waters of the quaint harbour came in sight, I breathed the words of a psalm, *thought* of saying, "I feel I want to cry" —and miraculously I felt calmer.

The remission didn't last, though I kept repeating the words of the psalm; but I stayed out of the lowest depths. An anti-depressant drug helped me greatly, and gradually I recovered my spirits and a degree of bodily wellbeing. In Cornwall again in the summer, I climbed the dizzy path from Porthcurno beach to the Minnack Theatre more quickly and less breathlessly than before my illness: I had done a lot of walking. I thanked God that I was almost out of the bad time. Reaching home, I plunged into writing a screenplay of *The White Hotel* and finished a draft in three weeks. I had scarcely been able to write a postcard until then.

Denise, Ross, and various animals, with furniture from her house, had settled in during my absence. It was very strange having the Muse so close at hand, doing my cooking, washing and ironing. It was strange for her having to look after a man. It would take time. We planned our delayed move to Cornwall.

The day after I'd finished the screenplay, I felt fluish and heavy in the legs. The fluishness and heavy-leggedness increased. I looked for something new to begin writing, but it was as if my brain had ground to a halt. There was nothing left to write or to live.

Misinterpreting a blood-test, I panicked. This ill feeling must be because my kidneys were failing. I called my doctor; dismissing my fears, she asked ironically was my body swelling up, was I terribly thirsty? Right after putting down the phone I developed a raging thirst and I could see my ankles and fingers swelling before my eyes. I rushed to London to see more dark-suited men. The first could find nothing wrong except bad varicose veins; he prescribed elastic stockings, thigh-length. But I didn't fancy wearing a suspender belt. The second, a highly-reputed Harley Street GP, diagnosed a renewal of depression. This took me aback; depression couldn't, surely, make one feel fluish and one's legs so heavy? I insisted on chest and spinal x-rays, which were done in the surgery. He would call me with the results next morning, he promised; he was sure they'd be clear. He recommended doubling my dose of anti-depressants.

Caitlin and Sean took me to see *Hannah and Her Sisters*. Watching Woody Allen's acute hypochondria, they said, "That's you, Dad!" And even I was forced to laugh. Next morning at Caitlin's flat I awaited the GP's phone call. It was late; I rang to enquire. He was busy, his assistant said; he would call within an hour.

I became hysterical. "That's it! There's something wrong in the x-rays. That's why I feel so weak! He's waiting until he's cleared his surgery, so that he can have a long talk with me. There's no other explanation. I've had it!"

Gulping her boyfriend's best malt whisky, I stared at a future in which I would be a permanent invalid. Or worse . . . No, on the whole, I preferred death.

When I'd drunk almost the whole bottle, the GP rang. The x-rays were clear, as expected; he'd talked to my consultants, and he was sticking to his diagnosis. "They're brilliant men. Okay, there's about a point nought nought one chance they've missed something . . . But that's really not very likely, is it?"

I embraced Caitlin drunkenly; then she drove me to consult a neurologist. Miraculously I responded to all the stimuli in the right way, and he said he thought I was just run down.

I came home unconvinced. The doubled anti-depressant didn't help. I saw a homeopath, who gave me little pills; three female faith healers worked me over. A heart specialist thought I was suffering from anxiety plus anti-depressants. A psychiatrist said it was atypical depression and anxiety, referring me to a psychotherapist.

"I know I'm bloody depressed!" I snarled at her. "I'm depressed because there's something physically wrong with me and they can't find out what! Or rather, they don't believe me."

Meanwhile Denise snarled because I was snarling and whining. Depression spreads. Even the cats became neurotic. I couldn't see anything ahead, anything worth living for. Every waking moment an intolerable strain, an abyss. *Sphinx* had anticipated mental distress, but I'd had no conception what it was like. I stared vacantly at soaps on daytime television and played endlessly a tape of *South Pacific*. It cheered me a little.

"You'll go mad," Denise warned.

I screamed, "I *am* mad! I *am* mad!"

My dreams were as terrible as my day-thoughts. I wasn't waking very early, like classic depressives, but sleeping on stupefied until nine or even ten. Always I struggled awake to the dinning hiss of tinnitus. I could only imagine my bad dreams were making it worsen during the night.

I had my first pleasant, hopeful dream for many weeks: I was at my old Australian High School, with Denise, but the school had become a comfortable hotel; broad, high windows looked out on a delightful green landscape. We strolled along streets with raised cobbled sidewalks lined with railings and brilliant hanging baskets of flowers. Picturesque and sun-drenched, with quaint steps and turnings, Melbourne seemed suddenly Mediterranean.

I suppose the sphinx of dreams was thinking partly of the Greek influence which had struck me forcibly on my visit to Melbourne in '84. She was recalling also happy holidays with Denise in Greece and Italy. But above all she seemed to be saying that all we needed for happiness was a complete change of scene. The circumstances, my circumstances, which had compelled us to live in a house full of ghosts were not propitious.

I became obsessed with the idea that if we went south of the equator all our problems, including my vague illness, would ease. It would be good, I thought, if Caitlin and Sean came too. A luxury holiday for us all, helping to heal wounds. But my plan didn't work out. Nothing was working out at this time. I flew south with my older children.

In the paradisal islands I was the same torpid body and hammering mind. Only distantly appreciative of the warmth, the sparkling sea and golden palm-fringed beaches, I sat gloomily, paced agitatedly on weak legs, or battered my children with hysterical alternatives for my miserable future. In seven days I drove them almost crazy and they developed a profound sympathy for and understanding of Denise, who had had to put up with this for several months.

The holiday did some good, in addition to that. They dragged me on to a tennis court, for the first time in ten years. Though I pulled a muscle and hobbled in agony for a couple of days, I had proved to myself that I could still stagger round a court for half-an-hour in extreme heat, so presumably I wasn't suffering from any dire physical condition. And for one hour, wading in the warm waters of an enchanted islet, I felt suddenly quite clear-headed and calm, without tinnitus or malaise: almost in a forgotten state of well-being.

"You're right and I'm wrong," I admitted; "it *is* mental."

"Thank God you're seeing sense," said Caitlin. "To an outsider it's so obviously psychosomatic—but you've never been able to see it. It's been breaking my heart to see you in such a state."

"Well, at least I know now. And it's a great relief."

The relief didn't outlast the evening. On the twelve-hour return flight I stared the whole time at the seat in front of me. When Ross, a computer-genius at ten, dives with a cormorant-flight on my new and totally baffling word-processor, the screen flashes with words and symbols which relay and rearrange themselves in a mad fashion. My brain was just such a screen on the flight—indeed at every moment of every day—going over and over the same real or imagined dilemmas, without any logical control.

In London I was to stay overnight at the Royal Great Western, Paddington—that familiar station of impossible choices. Sean, who usually deflects his strong feelings with drollery and wit, looked anxious, and insisted on carrying my case up to my bedroom. Surveying the drab room he said, "You won't do anything foolish, will you?" He could see me suspended on a tie from the ceiling. I assured him I felt too exhausted to commit suicide.

The months of hell dragged by, from autumn to spring. Perhaps hell changed gradually to purgatory. By now I was reasonably convinced it was all in my head, as the men in dark suits knew from the start. I could see the irony: I had written so much about psychosomatic and hysterical symptoms (as a defence against just such an attack, according to my therapist); yet I found it so hard to believe that my psyche was causing the pressure in my skull, making my legs feel as if they were wading through surf. I was, after all, of solid working-class Cornish stock, not from the Viennese *bourgeoisie*. Evidently this hadn't made me immune.

Totally incapable of writing, I also couldn't bear reading. Art terrified and disturbed me. At last I borrowed from the library the shortest novel I could find, Philip Roth's *The Ghost Writer*, and with a gigantic effort managed to get through it a few pages a day. It was in this book that I came across the quotation about 'the madness of art'.

My long-suffering GP sighed indulgently, as I said I'd like to consult just one more dark-suited man in London. The physician at St Thomas's listened very acutely to my case-history, and thought it was perhaps significant that my illness had fallen into two distinct phases.

He took blood, and a couple of weeks later found I had had glandular fever.

TWENTY-TWO

Archaeologies

Uncle Leslie turns up at 'Beverly' on Christmas Eve, bringing our presents. We see in his hands a plucked chicken. "The children's presents are in the chicken," he confides. The chicken is stowed in the oven. When the kitchen is empty, I creep to open the oven-door. Mother comes in. "Donald, what are you doing, dear?" "He said my present was in the chicken . . ."

With Donald Craze, the friend who was calling 'Shimmy-shirty!' when I broke my elbow, I play a timeless Test in the rough, cow-patted field behind our house. He is every member of the England team, batting and bowling, I am all the Australians under Bradman. We have intricate, careful score cards. Though the summer evening is still bright, Mum appears and says, "Donald, it's time to come in."

"Fuck."

A moment's astonishment, then: "Go to bed this instant!"

Abashed, bewildered, I go to my room and start undressing. What on earth does the word mean? It must be something very bad. When Dad comes home, he tells me I can get up and drive with him in the van up to Carnkie.

In winter, Saturday is always the best day. After the rugby we call into Auntie Nellie's sweet-shop for some sweets, then go to the pictures. Afterwards we stroll to Auntie Lilie's, where Mum has been visiting. Uncle Tommy always lifts his bum half off the chair and farts loudly; we laugh and Auntie Lilie, blushing, says, "Tommy!"

Late in the evening Dad and I walk to the railway station to wait for the Plymouth train bringing copies of the *Football Herald*. I shiver, from cold and from pleasurable anticipation at reading what they will say about Redruth's match. When the train has pulled in and we've bought the newspaper, we collect my mother and walk home. Tea and a saffron bun, with the crisp *Herald* spread out on the table. My father recalls, as a young man, walking home to Carnkie with the *Herald*, finding always a whole plate of saffron buns left by his mother. He reads, stretching for bun after bun, till his hand finds an empty plate.

One summer evening I read in the *News Chronicle* an item about a religious sect which believes the world will end next Saturday afternoon at five o'clock. The sect has taken to a mountain summit. I become filled with dread. To be so precise about the day and the hour—there must be something in it. No one else seems to have read the news item, and I tell no one about my fear. Saturday arrives, the last day; I go with school friends to a cricket match. But I can't enjoy it; no matter how many runs Redruth score, they won't have time to bowl the opposition out. After the tea interval, dread chokes me. I gaze beyond the white-clad scurrying players to the far boundary, expecting that it will soon be enveloped in a mist. The mist will engulf everything.

Wickets start to fall, and my attention is distracted back to the game. When I glance at the pavilion clock, it shows five-twenty. To my infinite relief, the world hasn't ended.

A weekday evening, behind the nets where we've been allowed to practise, boys in a pack surround me and pull me to the ground. They yank down my trousers and underpants. A gap opens for the stunted groundsman to peer at me, grinning. He doesn't do anything, just looks. They let me get to my feet and adjust my clothes. I walk home, trailing my bat, frightened and ashamed.

Whitsun Fair. I feel sick from the waltzers. A smooth-faced man starts to chat to me. He is saying something about spending a weekend with him somewhere. I shake my head and move away. Why should a stranger want to spend a weekend with me? Crazy!

Ah, these breasts! No wonder the three explorers gaze longingly at them across the burning desert! I know they are not quite like real breasts, which are rounded not conical; what moves me, I think, is that mountains can resemble breasts: even to their nipples of snow. And beyond them, I know well, is the descent into Solomon's diamond-mine . . . Shall I ever see such breasts? The illustration is magical; no matter how many times I read the book, always when I turn to this page my heart beats more rapidly, my fingers tremble.

It is with trepidation that I write this review of *Memories and Hallucinations*, since I am mentioned in it. I have to point out an inaccuracy in my portrayal; I am described as 'black old whiskery Thomas', whereas only my face is black; my body is chestnut-brown and I have white paws. But then, a great deal of the book is inaccurate; a refining censor has been at work; there is no mention of the times I was left shivering out in the rain because of some row going on—whether over something trivial, such as the woe that is in marriage, or important, such as who should open our tin of food.

The author attempts a kind of walkabout through parts of his life. There is no particular pattern to these walks; he could surely learn from the precise track we beat down through the wintry neglected lawn. He deals almost in the same haphazard way with some aspects of his writings, more than once quoting a Henry James character on 'the madness of art'. He offers extracts from an indeterminate analysis, which makes me grateful I am only the third syllable of Oedipus and have been neutered.

There are inexplicable omissions. Where, for example, is Marmaduke—perhaps my brother—who lorded it over the garden for almost ten years? I see him plodding indomitably across the grass, returning from some nocturnal escapade, a torn ear flapping. Matchless in personality, he isn't even granted a mention!

In short, I can't recommend this book.

When I learned I had had glandular fever, I felt angry with my analyst. The guilty virus is notorious for lingering around and bringing on depression—even when the illness has been diagnosed, as mine had not been. I thought of all the time and money I had wasted, when it was my body that was responsible, not my mind. Urged to accept that my whole organism had been under attack, I found it strangely hard to do so. That was okay for Freud's hysterics, but I was different.

Gradually, as I began to feel I might not forever be doomed to malaise, creative deadness and despair, I acknowledged that the hours spent with my therapist weren't wasted; that she was my necessary guide through a second nightmarish dreamtime in my life. As at 15, so at 51, a grim journey towards—I hoped—self-discovery.

The only benefit of a depression, and perhaps its purpose, is that it allows you to explore your dreamtime. American Indians go into the desert to find their dreamsong, their personal song which guarantees their survival. A Papago woman remarked: "Our song is short because we know so much." I know little.

Or as my guide puts it, "We have begun to explore the causes. There isn't just one thing. You've built an immense, complex defensive structure, trying to bring shape, virtue and goodness out of disturbing, difficult material. Some of which you have incorporated into your way of viewing life. And at times you just wish you could sit comfortably inside it still, don't you? Of course it's easy to see what brought the whole thing crashing down; but that was just a step along the way; the whole thing is as deep as a mine."

Outstretched, attentive, I am also standing in the kitchen of my childhood, near the door, watching my father grappling with Lois, trying to make her give him a kiss. I've been explaining to my analyst the geography of our tiny bungalow, how one could see from the kitchen into my sister's bedroom when the doors were open. Mother is near me, working, and calling to Lois, "Don't be so cold to your father—give him a hug."

I am moved by the waywardness, the apparent randomness, of memory. I have no memories relating to my own tiny bedroom, next to my sister's, except of the moment when I coughed up milk into my mother's lap; yet I slept there for twelve years. Memory, like the events it randomly records —such as Lois being 'cold' to her father, and Mother scolding her—can't be struggled with, or analysed. It's the way it is. And a memory, in its relative haziness, its dreamlike inevitability, may be a truer reflection of events than one's experience of them at the time.

Lois too must have that feeling, when she looks back on the journeys of her life, from California to Cornwall to Melbourne to California: that they happened like memories.

She is in my thoughts, because she has phoned me from Glasgow, having flown across the Atlantic to visit her son. Since a return to Cornwall is one of many options in her life, she is anxious to see my Cornish cottage. It will be nice to see me too, if I can meet her there.

"It's time."

Denise and I sat with her, drinking coffee and eating Cornish fudge. She enthused over the open-plan ground floor, with its granite fireplace and its minstrels' gallery. It is sparely furnished, its shelves crowded with a spillover of unwanted books from Hereford: unread novels sent by hopeful publishers, and unreadable foreign-language editions of my own books.

Her voice was American, though an expert might have detected hints of Australia and Cornwall. This was only our third brief meeting in thirty-six years. At sixty-two, her vivacity is unabated; she has matured into a merry, yet deeply spiritual, widow. In her frequent references to God, as a friend and neighbour, I could hear my mother's voice. Her auburn hair had turned grey, increasing the resemblance.

"Well—were they happy?" I asked abruptly.

"Oh, I think so. Don't you?"

"I *thought* so."

We giggled, almost like brother and sister.

Although, she said, he had that melancholy look. A look

that suggested frustration. "Mum thought it was enough to be pretty."

We wondered if he had been in love with Mona. Was that the secret of Restronguet? We agreed it would be difficult not to be in love with Mona. We had called on her and found her, at seventy-five, as irrepressibly funny as ever.

"It was Dad who wanted you desperately," Lois said. "Mum wasn't so keen, but Dad persuaded her not to put all her eggs in one basket. Of course, once she had you, she was all over you."

"My analyst thinks I felt very excluded."

"Are you crazy? It was *I* who felt excluded!"

We giggled again.

"You were always in bed with them."

"From the first?"

She nodded. "You would cry, and in you'd go with them and then Pam, our evacuee, had your bedroom for four years. Remember?"

"No."

Did I recall when there was a terrible thunderstorm and we were all four in bed together? A memory, fainter than the faintest sheet-lightning, stirred. "You were in their bed," she said, "and Dad called out to me, 'Come and join us!' I called back, 'You'll have to come and get me!' So he did."

For a time, he had been quite obsessional about her.

We took a drive. At the corner, opening into the village square, she admired a Celtic cross. The early saints and traders from Ireland and Wales passed through St Erth on their way to Brittany. Something holy lingered here.

I drove up the motorway to Redruth, slowing a little, as I usually did, outside 'Beverly'. The 'For Sale' sign I'd noticed last autumn had gone; Mona had told us the owners were prevented from selling because there was a shaft under the bungalow. We couldn't believe that our skilful and careful father had built his own home over a shaft.

Someone had had the front lawn concreted. Otherwise, as Lois remarked, it looked much the same. But of course it wasn't. I took the hill towards Carnkie. "Stop," she said, outside 'St Martin's'. Here the elegant Edwardian garden, secluded with shrubs and privet, had been replaced by garages and work-sheds. We gazed like archaeologists. It was deeper than Troy.

When Denise, Ross and I returned to Hereford, we were puzzled to see my piece of Athenian marble on the front step. I feared telekinetic activity; and the marble had sombre over-tones. "What's this doing here?" I asked Caitlin, opening the door to us.

"Oh, I just wanted something to hold down the milk money."

"Hold down the milk money! The Acropolis was built with that marble."

"Oh!" She giggled. "Sorry!"

I go to my study, to the still-virginal word processor. I switch on. The screen floods with emerald, like the sea off the Logan Stone.

Where shall we sail?

I had no idea. The waters were still murky. We thought we had bought a house in Truro, but the sale fell through. Just as I was beginning to regain my health and spirits, misfortune fell on my son in London. But first he had good fortune: his novel was accepted by a publisher. Then he was falsely accused of a crime, was refused bail, and was thrown into Wormwood Scrubs. His suffering was mine; I couldn't bear his loss of freedom. I looked at our two fragments of Athenian marble; there seemed to have been constant ill luck ever since I had been given them. I put them in a plastic bag; I walked down the avenue to the tow-path, took the white stones from the bag and threw them into the river.

November. The leaves brushing against my analyst's consult-ing room window are red and gleaming under a cold blue sky.

"The timing of this move of yours," she says, "—apart from the practical questions of the right house at the right time, and so on—has something to do with this analysis. You're afraid of our closeness, of our becoming close. On one of the few occasions here when you've shown emotion, you called me austere. A cold cow."

"Did I say that?"

"Yes. And your fear of our closeness is of course indicative of much broader feelings. Your fear goes back deep, deep."

"To my mother?"

"Yes. For whatever reason, relating to her own background, she couldn't give you the closeness, the warmth, the abundance of love which you needed."

"But surely, in that case, I should have a fear of *un*closeness, distance, rather than closeness?"

"No, you reacted by cutting off feelings, denying your need . . . It's very complex, I'm having to condense and not wait for the appropriate time to tell you things because you're leaving. Some of it won't make real sense for a while yet . . ."

Her calm and somehow rather tender voice washes over me. I lie and take it: at one point cupping my chin in my hands almost as if in prayer. I think of my beloved mother playing hopscotch in the field near her cottage, twenty years before I was born. I feel that I'm pleasantly floating.

"Is it time?"

"Yes."

I check myself from saying "*Pora!*—It's time!" Swinging off the couch, I bury my head in my hands.

"Jesus!"

Between the consulting room and the front door I turn and say, "You're not austere! Not a cold cow!" In her austere face her eyes are warm.

"See you Thursday." And I surprise myself by giving her a wink.